"So no dinner for guys in black hats, huh?"

"Nope." Jessica rocked back on her heels, looking rather proud of herself.

Adam studied her for a long time, wondering about all that pent-up energy, and then finally shook his head. "Now you've done it. You're an insurmountable challenge, Barnes."

For a heartbeat their gazes were locked. He could see it in her eyes: the challenge, the excitement. She loved the game just as much as he did.

"Just don't get any ideas about *surmounting,* if you get *my* drift, Taylor."

"Hey, you get your mind out of those dark, sexy places you don't want to go to, and I'll do the same."

She stared him down, the glasses tapping against her thigh. "You're no threat to my peace of mind...only to my career ambitions."

He laughed softly. "I'm going to go have dinner, Barnes. You're welcome to join me."

She turned and walked away, a cocky swing in her hips. "In your dreams, Taylor." She tossed the words over her shoulder.

"There, too, Barnes. There, too."

Dear Reader,

All through my life I've been lucky enough to count among my friends some of the most extraordinary women in the entire universe. Some of the friendships have lasted forever, while others are more recent, but in the truest sort of friendships, years are simply relative and most often just get in the way. There is no stronger bond than the friendship between women. It is forged through the hot steel of shared suffering and stupid mistakes, and then cooled over time until only the bond remains. The years pass, marriages and children struggle and pull at the friendship, but it never breaks. Like the indomitable will of women, it will endure. Always.

Kathleen

P.S. I love to hear from readers. If you'd like to write, my address is P.O. Box 312, Nyack, NY 10960, or visit my Web site: www.kathleenoreilly.com.

Books by Kathleen O'Reilly

HARLEQUIN TEMPTATION
889—JUST KISS ME
927—ONCE UPON A MATTRESS

HARLEQUIN DUETS
66—A CHRISTMAS CAROL

KATHLEEN O'REILLY

PILLOW TALK

TORONTO • NEW YORK • LONDON
AMSTERDAM • PARIS • SYDNEY • HAMBURG
STOCKHOLM • ATHENS • TOKYO • MILAN • MADRID
PRAGUE • WARSAW • BUDAPEST • AUCKLAND

To Jill, Lynn, Stacy, Sara, Nedra, Marian, Tanja, Meyerer, Martha, Suzanne, Marsha, Julia, Dee and Sherry.

ISBN 0-373-69167-X

PILLOW TALK

Copyright © 2004 by Kathleen Panov.

This edition published by arrangement with Harlequin Books S.A.

Visit us at www.eHarlequin.com

Printed in U.S.A.

1

JESSICA BARNES studied the bride critically. Perfect. The warm, sparkling, spring afternoon was a rare thing in Chicago. White flowers covered the arbor, not one dead blossom in sight. The musicians hadn't missed a note. The slim branches from the weeping willow trees danced in the gentle breeze. Absolutely perfect.

Yup, there was nothing like seeing fairy-tale happiness to make you feel like crap. "Do you think she's put on weight since college?"

Safe on the far side of the garden, far away from the white, flower-strewn tent, the four friends shook their heads. It was a sad day for them all.

Mickey was the most practical. "It's the dress. All those ruffles. I don't know why women don't understand the illusion of substance that ruffles project." She shook her head and made a note in her PalmPilot.

Jessica considered her own well-stocked closet, completely ruffle-free. She didn't have the fashion sense of Dior, but she managed.

Beth sighed, her eyes still locked on the groom. A long, wistful sigh that she did so well. "He looks pretty good. Kenny never looked that good." Kenny was Beth's ex. An ex they'd never liked, but that was the sort of thing you didn't tell your friends. Subtle hints, yes. Life-damaging proclamations, no.

Cassandra, never one to confess weakness, studied her nails. Ten perfect ovals trimmed in Scarlet Nights. "He asked me out once, but I said 'no.' I was in my medical-students-only stage."

"Kenny asked you out?" Beth's wide blue eyes looked horrified.

Cassandra exhaled, her white sheath lifting gracefully. "No. Charles, the *groom*."

"She looks happy," Mickey put in, veering the subject away from No-Account Kenny.

Beth swallowed one bite of the wedding cake before licking the crumbs from her lip. "She's glowing."

That met with a long, jealous silence. They might as well just brand the lot of them with a scarlet *L*.

"Who needs love?" Cassandra asked, and then took a healthy drink of champagne.

Beth never took her eyes off the happy couple. "I do."

With a bit more violence than finesse, Jessica speared the olive in her drink. This was an argument they'd had many times. "No, Beth, you don't. You're a single woman with your independence, you can stay up as late as you want, let the laundry stack up, go to happy hour whenever you choose. What's not to love?" Just to prove her point, she swallowed the olive whole, a gesture her freshman-year fiancé had abhorred. They had broken up soon after.

Beth defended herself. "Sometimes it's lonely."

"Get a cat," Mickey said.

Was a cat everyone's answer to life? Jessica just shook her head. "Oh, please, no. Aunt Charisse had ten cats when she died. They could *not* get the smell out of the carpet. Ever. Finally replaced the carpet, the padding, even deodorized the slab, and still they had to take ten K off the price."

Mickey raised her sunglasses and studied the bride once more. They'd all gone to college with Annie Summers, and now, six years after graduation, Annie was the first to get married. Second if you counted Beth's two-week marriage, but they usually didn't count Kenny. "I think white just isn't her color. She should have done something with a rose tone for her complexion, don't you think?"

"I heard they're going to the Caribbean for the honeymoon." Beth studied the hors d'oeuvre on the side table, finally settling for the curried shrimp.

"That's so cliché."

"I want to go to the Canadian Rockies on my honeymoon." Beth sounded as though she was reciting a Christmas list. Jessica wanted to shake her sometimes, tell her the world wasn't one big Disney movie, but she never did. Instead, they did their best to protect Beth from ever learning that Disney owned Miramax, too.

"Why don't you go by yourself?" Cassandra asked.

Beth froze, her blue eyes wide. "I could, couldn't I?"

Mickey shrugged. "Sure."

"I don't know. If I went now, where would I go on my honeymoon?" Beth sounded so certain. As if honeymoons were part of life's guarantees. Jessica was much more realistic. There were no guarantees, unless you did it yourself.

"What if you don't *ever* get married again?" Always the troublemaker, Cassandra wouldn't let it drop.

"Cassandra, don't scare the girl," Jessica said, working to avoid a scene.

"She doesn't need a man," Cassandra insisted.

Jessica just rolled her eyes at that. "Big words from a woman who always has a date on Saturday night."

After one regal sniff, Cassandra went on. "No, I'm serious. I could remain single for the rest of my life and be happy."

Mickey raised a hand, sans ring. "I could, too."

Beth stood firm. "Not me. I want to get married."

Jessica raised her glass. "To the solo state of mind. Junk food and chick flicks forever. A bachelorette pact, single forever."

Mickey and Cassandra clinked glasses. "Hear, hear."

By the look on her face, Beth knew she was defeated. After a long moment of silence, she joined in. "Screw 'em all."

Cassandra laughed, that throaty laugh she had perfected over the years. "Honey, life isn't long enough."

Sometimes marriage was overrated, but Jessica knew the truth. They had been single for so long that it was now easier to attack the institution of marriage than to face failure. Jessica hated failure.

"Marriage is nothing more than a woman's subjugation to a man's need for dominance. Ha. They try and dominate me, I'll pin the laser on them." Mickey worked at a research lab and had never yet met a man, or anyone for that matter, with a higher IQ.

Jessica speared another olive. "You know, there are some advantages to marriage. Actually, ever since the government tinkered with the tax structure, it doesn't cost as much as it used to. For instance, I would probably jump into the next tax bracket, assuming he's a white-collar professional; however, I'd get a credit of almost eight thousand. Not a great investment, but I suppose if he's willing to cook every now and then, it could be worth it." Jessica hated to cook.

"Or you could take all that money you'd put in extra taxes and buy your Porsche."

That earned a smile. Only 2.1 more years and then the Porsche would be hers. Unless she got the promotion to vice president at Hard-Wire Networks, a computer networking equipment manufacturer. Not likely, but possible. The raise would put her in Porsche-attainment status within nine months.

"Now you've done it," Mickey said with a sigh. "She's going to have an orgasm, right here."

Of course, if Adam Taylor had his evil way, she wouldn't be polishing a Porsche, she'd be polishing her résumé. The impending buyout made her nervous, made her cranky and worst of all, made her sneeze. First her nose tickled, then twitched, and finally she began to wheeze.

Mickey started to laugh.

Jessica blew her nose and sniffed—for effect not necessity. "Orgasm? Not all of us have Cassandra's talents."

Cassandra's smile spoke volumes. "All you have to do is exercise."

Mickey waved a languid hand and assumed a Southern drawl. "I abhor exercise. I need my cabana-boy to do it for me."

"*He* could be my cabana-boy," Cassandra said with a nod to the other side of the garden.

Yes indeed, when it came down to men, they were all such frauds. Jessica, Mickey and Beth turned to look. Mickey and Beth got that gooey look. Jessica simply wanted to hit something.

He was here. *Adam Taylor.*

And didn't that just put a cherry on top of the day? Tall, impossibly handsome in a dark suit, and worst of all—intelligent, witty, sharp. That brought her thoughts to a halt. Sharp like an executioner's ax.

She shouldn't have been surprised; the groom worked at Adam's firm, after all.

Life really wasn't fair. Work had been hell for her since he arrived, a consultant brought in by JCN, the international computer conglomerate, to prepare a report on Hard-Wire's buyout potential. An "operational efficiency expert."

Yeah, you could call 'em all the pretty terms you

wanted, but you still couldn't disguise that chainsaw. She picked up an olive and popped it in her mouth.

He turned and saw her, favoring her with a cool, appraising gray-green stare. Jessica was grateful for her sunglasses. She could *look* as if she was calm and in control. But then her nose began to twitch and she sneezed. Twice. She searched her pockets for a tissue, but came up empty. Great.

When she looked up, Mickey was still eyeing Adam with appreciation. Jessica felt inclined to enlighten them all. "He's okay, if you like the rich, strong, arrogant jerks."

"You know him?" Mickey asked smoothly.

Jessica bit into her last olive. "Adam Taylor," she mumbled between bites.

They had all listened to Jessica's horror stories of Mr. Adam "The Ax-Man" Taylor, but she'd never described him physically. It seemed a betrayal to her lifelong ambition of job security and Porsche ownership. Adam was the enemy.

"He wants you," Cassandra said, swirling her glass.

"In your dreams," Jessica answered, not wanting to discuss her own dreams about Adam. Mr. Taylor. The Ax-Man.

"If you smile, I bet he'll come over," Beth said, trying to make the world a happier place. And failing.

"Not if I leave first."

"Jessica, Jessica, I never thought I'd see you playing the coward. Tsk, tsk," Cassandra teased.

The coward remark was really a low blow, but not

enough to divert Jessica from her plan. "I needed to leave early anyway."

Mickey raised a brow. "And that's why we all came in one car?"

She was outnumbered. Three to one. "You're supposed to be my friends."

"Friends don't let friends run away," Cassandra said, pushing her in the direction of her worst nightmare. And her steamiest dream.

"He can't be that bad. He's got a nice smile," Beth said, still permanently fixed in Pollyanna-land.

"Tell that to Red Riding Hood's grandmother."

"Go on. What can it hurt?" Mickey said, completely practical.

Jessica popped another olive in her mouth and adjusted her sunglasses, the picture of aloof sophistication. She spoiled it all with a sneeze.

CHARLES WAS a stuffed-shirt prick, but Adam had learned long ago never to burn a bridge. They had worked together on the Symtheson-Hardwick buyout, growth in revenue: $4.7 million over five years, total jobs lost: 537. The consulting firm they worked for, Kearney, Markham and Williams, considered that a very good deal indeed.

On most days, Adam ignored the consequences of his work. He was a consultant. Get in, make recommendations, get out. He was good at what he did and life treated him right.

He sipped his champagne and glanced around for a

beer. He'd never liked champagne, but always took a glass at social functions. Of course, most of it ended up watering the potted plants.

Charles caught his eye and Adam pasted a "How the hell you doing?" smile on his face. He had more friends than the president, every one his best buddy, but he couldn't remember the last time he felt the desire to talk with anyone about subjects other than the market, the weather or golf. Golf was the worst. He shot a seventy-three and hated the game.

He moved into virtual consultant mode and strolled over to where the happy couple was eyeing each other with pure rose-colored lust. Envy seared him, hot and fast. For a moment he dropped his guard, and thought about his house in Alabama. His empty house. He closed his eyes and counted to eleven. By the time he reached the end of the exercise, the consultant was back.

He clapped Charles on the shoulder. "You lucky dog," he said, more truth than not.

The groom slipped an arm around his new wife. "Hands off, Taylor. According to the laws of this fine state, she's all mine."

First compliment the client and then on to more trivial topics. "And you picked a gorgeous day to marry a gorgeous woman."

Annie blushed, and planted a soft kiss on Adam's cheek. "Thank you, Adam."

Charles lifted his glass. "Blue skies, my friend. All blue skies. Hey, I see you've been assigned Hard-

Wire. Sweet deal. Read the report. Lots of opportunity for efficiency there."

Translation: We could trim fifteen percent and the company would never miss it.

"Too early to tell," Adam answered.

Translation: Yeah, that's what I'm thinking. Maybe twenty.

Charles nodded toward the far garden. "You met Jessica Barnes yet? She's manager of finance there. She went to school with Annie. If you haven't met her, you should let Annie introduce you. She could really show you the ropes."

Translation: Play your cards right, two dinners and a movie, and you'll get laid.

Adam turned and let his gaze linger on Jessica. Yeah, he knew her. She was one of the fifteen to twenty percent. Great legs, savvy and a dark glare that said never trust her with sharp objects nearby. Undomesticated and ambitious.

Translation: Trouble.

For two weeks, Adam had worked himself into a serious frenzy to keep from personalizing Jessica Barnes. Personalizing was a bad thing to do in his line of work. He avoided looking at her in meetings, and thought of her as her employee number—44713, never Jessica. But he'd be a stupid man not to realize that 44713 lit up buttons he didn't even know he had.

Damn it all to hell, he'd never been stupid.

He watched her pick her way through the crowd, passing between pastel suits and wide-brimmed hats and men in dark tuxes. Today she'd worn neon blue. He'd spent more time than he liked to admit wondering what sort of clothes 44713 wore out of the office. Monday through Friday, eight to five, she was so tightly buttoned. Prim and proper, never a false step.

Except when she sneezed.

That brought a smile to his face. He pretended to sip his champagne and watched the sun beat down on her thick, brown hair. She'd let it slip down around her shoulders today. Adam normally liked blondes, but he'd never seen brown hair that caught the sunlight so well, or looked so temptingly touchable.

A man could weave fantasies that involved that hair.

She finally reached his side, dark sunglasses hiding her eyes. Soft brown. Gold and green swirled together in darkness. "Hello, Taylor. I didn't expect to see you here today. I thought you'd be at Hard-Wire doing inventory."

He winced. 44713. 44713. It made his job easier. "Lovely day, don't you think?"

"A good day for a wedding."

"You know Annie?"

"School. You?"

"Charles is one of our auditors."

"Imagine that. Small world."

Too small. Way, way too small when he started having thoughts that involved one of his client's employees. Thoughts of long sleepless nights in bed and hot showers that had nothing to do with hygiene.

Fantasies.

For two years a lonely reality had honed his expectation. He wanted a wife. A family. White-picket fences and apple pie.

Jessica Barnes—44713—was not potential wife material. Her potential was purely sensual, and he felt it oozing through every inch of her sun-kissed skin.

"Why don't you come out to dinner with me this evening?" said the spider to the fly. The words were out of his mouth before he thought.

"Sorry. I'm tied up."

The fly had brains. "Pity. Tomorrow?"

"Mr. Taylor, I don't think it's wise for us to consider anything more than a strictly business relationship."

He completely agreed with her logic. In fact, he'd thought of it himself. However, something about her legs made logic impossible. "Ms. Barnes, you work for one company, I work for another. There's no legal, moral or ethical reason you couldn't have dinner with me. Unless that's your choice?"

She didn't even hesitate to skewer his ego. "Of course that's my choice." She turned to walk away from him, and he nearly dropped his glass. Her entire back was bare. Tan, smooth, with a long, long line that ran down from smooth shoulders and dipped low and lower still.

He couldn't help himself. He reached out and traced one wayward finger down the delectable curve. Hands-on usually wasn't his style: he'd always believed it was only polite to wait until you're invited to touch.

But he'd never seen a back like that before.

She froze.

"Jessica."

She didn't turn, just stood there, flaunting all that silky skin. His mouth grew dry and his mind kicked in with all sorts of images that involved skin and touching. Mouths. Tangled legs.

"It's only going to get worse," he said, more to himself than to her.

"What is?"

"Seeing each other, every day, being polite and completely professional."

Then she spun around. Stared up at him, those soulless glasses giving nothing away. "I can handle it."

He almost argued with her, saying that *he* couldn't. He, the consummate professional. The man who could finesse anything. But he didn't. Now wasn't the time.

A smattering of applause started in the crowd. They both turned to look. Annie and Charles made their way to the main table. "Hope they're one of the lucky fifty percent," she murmured.

"Actually, they only need to be one of the lucky seventy-five percent."

The sunglasses came off then, the brown eyes alight. "No, that's not right. According to the census bureau it's fifty percent."

She was always so passionate about being right, even when she was wrong. Adam had seen her operate in meetings, found himself stepping in when he shouldn't. All to protect 44713.

Jessica.

What was it about her? He shrugged his shoulders. He wasn't going to analyze it, just go with it.

But he hid his smile because he wasn't stupid. "No, you can't say that. I stand by my seventy-five. Seventy-five percent of the married people in this country have never been divorced."

She shook her head, brown hair flying. "You're wrong, Taylor."

"Want to bet on that?"

"What?"

"You name the stakes. A cup of coffee…money." He eyed her mouth. "A kiss."

She pursed her lips. Today she wore more lipstick than usual. Dark maroon, the color of heart, the color of sin. "No kisses, Taylor. One dollar."

What harm could come from a bet? He could almost hear his mother's lecture about gambling, but he'd think about that later. "We can settle this tomorrow at the office, or if you want, we could leave right now and find the answer."

"I don't trust you."

She was smart. People shouldn't trust him. "Sorry you feel that way."

"You're wearing the black hat, Taylor. That's the way it is."

"So, no dinner for guys in black hats, huh?"

"Nope." She rocked back on her heels, looking rather proud of herself.

He studied her for a long time, wondering about all that pent-up energy, and then finally he shook his head. "Now you've done it. You're an insurmountable challenge, Barnes."

For three heartbeats, their gazes locked. He could see it in her eyes, the challenge, the excitement. She loved the game just as much as he did. Eventually she looked away. "Just don't get any ideas about surmounting, if you get my drift."

"You get your mind out of those dark places you don't want to go to, and I'll get mine out of there as well."

She stared him down, the glasses tapping against her thigh. "You're no threat to my peace of mind, only to my career ambitions."

He laughed softly. "I've had enough of this finger food. I'm going to go have dinner, Barnes. You're welcome to join me."

She turned and walked away, a cocky swing in her hips. "In your dreams, Taylor," she tossed over her shoulder.

"There, too, Barnes. There, too."

2

ON MONDAY, Jessica arrived at work at 7:00 a.m. sharp. She tried to stay busy, reading over the third-quarter forecast, marking the items that seemed questionable. Better analyzing numbers than staring at her computer and analyzing Saturday's skin-tickling encounter with Adam.

Mr. Taylor.

The Ax-man.

She needed to keep him in perspective, but he made perspective very difficult.

Needing a distraction, she read all her e-mail, accepted Mickey's lunch invitation, and just when she was done, one last message made it through.

Jessica,
Do you have the preliminary numbers for the third-quarter forecast? Could you drop it by my office?

Adam

She tapped her fingers on the keyboard. Office? Whose office? Last she'd heard, his team would be using the conference room at the corner of the building. She fired off her reply.

Adam,
Whose office?

Jessica

In a few seconds, she heard the incoming e-mail chime.

Jessica,
Look out your window.

Adam

Nooo.

She turned and stared out her window that faced into the interior of the building. Sure enough, across the atrium, directly in her line of vision, stood Adam. Without a jacket. Looking wonderfully awake and full of pep. He waved at her.

She waved back. With all the enthusiasm of a turkey in November.

He wanted the preliminary third-quarter figures? Fine. She printed out a copy of the spreadsheet that she'd put together, took a cup of coffee and made her way to his office.

His door was open, so she didn't bother to knock. She noted that he had been given one of the bigger offices, bigger than hers. Petty, very petty, but still it ticked her off. Jessica put the paper down on his desk and turned to leave.

"Miss Barnes, just a minute. I have some questions," he said, the hint of some genteel Southern upbringing in his voice.

Of course he had questions. Jessica pulled up a chair and took a sip of hot coffee. That improved her mood significantly. She hadn't been sleeping well recently. Mostly worrying about her job, but every now and then those steamy dreams reared their prurient heads. Those were the ones that made her nervous.

She slid an inch away from him. Not that it helped. She could still smell his cologne, could still feel his warmth, even from where she sat. Just to be safe, she slid an inch farther.

As if he knew her thoughts, Adam turned his head and looked at her.

She smiled in return, a smile that wasn't going to reach her eyes, but she was determined to make the effort. Be professional.

Then he fired off his questions. How comfortable was she with the European prospects? Did they consider the number from the telecommunications sector viable? Each time he asked, she answered, confident of the data.

At long last, he leaned back in his chair, apparently satisfied. "You do a great job."

She nodded her head, acknowledging the compliment. She had worked her rear off to get where she was. At last she had found a place where she belonged, a place where she could do something good. It was easy to do a great job now. "I've been at Hard-Wire since the early days of the product plan. I don't want anything to happen to this company."

Her nose began to tickle and she held up a finger, before eventually the sneeze erupted. He handed her a tissue.

"Like the possible acquisition." It wasn't a question.

She stuffed the tissue in her pocket, stalling more than anything. There was a time for honesty and a time for tact. Carefully she studied his face, his cool eyes expressionless. Eventually she shrugged. Honesty was her style. "Yes. JCN is too big and cumbersome. Hard-Wire will lose its competitive edge. The speed to market."

"But JCN can give you the brand name and stable image you need."

Jessica stiffened her spine. She had heard the rationale. "We shouldn't be having this discussion."

"Probably not, but I'm interested in why you're so opposed. Everyone else is walking around with a satisfied smile, planning for that new car they're hoping to buy." He took a pen and tapped it on the desk, the sound carrying in the quiet room. "Sounds like a disconnect to me. Maybe you see something that JCN doesn't."

Jessica stood, coffee in hand. Retreat was the best solution. "I'll leave now."

"Before you go, I've got one more thing."

"What?"

"Our bet." He pulled out a thick, leather-bound volume. "I'm assuming you'll believe the U.S. government?"

She hedged, staring at the defeat he held in his hand. "Not always."

"There." He opened the book to the bookmark and ran one finger down to the middle of the page. She edged behind him, trying to ignore his cologne, trying to pretend she wasn't studying the thick dark waves that settled so nicely against his neck. "Seventy-five percent of those people who are married have never been divorced. People who've been divorced tend to get divorced again. It's a common misinterpretation of the actual facts."

When he turned in his chair, she realized she was closer than comfort demanded. His arm brushed against her leg, just a touch, probably an accident. An accident that nearly spilled her coffee. She took a long, steadying breath. Easy, girl.

"I owe you a dollar. I don't have one with me, but I'll make sure you're paid before the end of the day."

His smile turned sly. "You can owe me."

She wanted to be offended. She wanted to step back and play the outraged female. But her nerve endings had plans of their own. Still and frozen, she was determined to persevere. "You win this round, Taylor."

For a moment his eyes softened. "You like to win, don't you, Barnes?"

She'd lost one too many times in her life. "Everyone does."

Then the shutters fell, the softness was gone. "A class act knows when to throw in the towel, too."

He meant Hard-Wire. He meant preparing for the inevitable. But for her that meant defeat. First they'd have to pry the office badge from her cold, dead hands. She sneezed. "I'll take the next round."

The arrogant man shrugged. "If there is a next round."

"Of course there will be. Good day, Mr. Taylor." She turned to leave, slamming the door behind her.

JESSICA'S 11:00 A.M. staff meeting dragged on forever. She couldn't wait to escape the confines of the building, and lunch with Mickey would go a long way to reestablishing her peace of mind.

She hoped.

When she made it to the small burger place just outside the Loop, Mickey was already seated. After they ordered, the talk was innocent and free of Mickey's mind tricks. They discussed her new project at the research lab, the Cubs, and made plans for the weekend. Just when Jessica started to relax, blitzkrieg began.

"You're uptight, J. More so than usual. It's Taylor, isn't it?"

Jessica chose the easy answer. "He's the enemy, Mick. JCN." Her voice fell soft. "They'd eliminate my position. Strike that—they'd eliminate the whole finance department."

"You don't know that. Besides, the stock options would help you weather the storms."

Jessica knew she'd make a little money on a buyout, but that was small comfort. She wanted VP. And her experience wasn't strong enough to be VP at anyplace but Hard-Wire. Being without a job, talking to head-hunters, networking. The whole process put a huge rock in her stomach.

And made her sneeze. She searched her purse for a tissue.

Mickey held up a French fry, analyzing it before popping it into her mouth. "I don't think you should go out with him."

"Why not?"

"Office romance. Bad for your image."

Jessica knew that. Seeing Adam personally, in any capacity, on a date or in his bed, could end up a CLM—career-limiting move. "I know," she said, still dwelling on the "in his bed" image.

Mickey snagged another fry. "Bet he's a jerk."

A jerk? Those misty green eyes of his weren't full of jerkiness. Every now and then he lowered his shields and she saw something else. Sadness? "Not really. He seems more remote than anything."

"Maybe he's from New York. That would explain it."

"No. He's from somewhere in the South. Can't figure out where."

Mickey drew a double helix in the ketchup. "The South? New York would have been better. Your allergies would go ballistic."

Jessica sneezed. "Thank you, oh brilliant one."

"Hey, I call 'em like I see 'em."

"What would you do? Would you gamble your professional image on a question mark?"

"J, there are two sorts of men in the world. Ethyl alcohol and nitric acid. The ethyl alcohol is a steady reliable fuel, doesn't burn clean, but it always burns. When you need to get there, positively, in three days—ethyl alcohol. And then there's nitric acid. It won't always fire, but when it does? To the moon, baby. You've got to make the decision: alcohol or nitric."

Jessica pulled the tissue through her hands. "I'm getting too old for nitric acid."

Mickey shrugged. "Your decision."

"There's not one good reason I should go for it." She had thought about it for some time. Fourteen days to be exact. Hot sex, although tempting, was not rational or logical given the situation. So why was she still thinking about it?

Mickey's laugh was the evil laugh of a mind reader. "I can see it's pointless to argue. You want him? Do him."

"No, no, no. I don't need the additional stress."

"Yes, I can see you're the picture of relaxed self-contemplation."

Jessica buried her head in her hands. "Forty-seven days and then he'll be gone. I just have to resist him for forty-seven days."

"How long has it been?"

"Fourteen." Her nose tickled, giving her its own opinion. One, two, three. *Ha-choo.*

"Then you might as well throw in the towel now, because I'm figuring within another week, you'll either be having a seriously good time with Mr. Taylor, or else you'll be buried alive under a mountain of shredded tissue."

Jessica stared at the little bits of paper that were littered across the table like broken dandelions. The histamines had won.

SOMETIMES Adam drove to the high-rise office park on Monroe that housed Hard-Wire, sometimes he took the El. On the long assignments, he kept his car with him. The car kept him from getting lonely.

Lonely. His mom would have a field day with that. He could just hear her.

You wouldn't be lonely if you'd just settle down. All that travel, one of these days your plane is going to crash and then where will you be?

"Up in heaven with you, Ma," he answered aloud. An automatic reply.

Pretty words never worked on me. I raised you, boy. I taught you everything you know.

He laughed at that and took a right-hand turn into traffic.

Cancer had buried his mother two years ago and it was only now that the sadness was starting to give way. He liked driving in the car and feeling as though she was there. Some days when the loneliness hit him hard, he talked to her aloud. Just like in *Psycho*. Which didn't worry him as much as it should. But he kept the secret to himself because he knew nobody else would understand.

Of course, now his conscience sounded just like his ma. At least he'd always assumed it was his conscience.

The cell phone beeped and he looked at the caller ID to see if he wanted to be available. Vanessa Green.

He let it go for two rings, weighing the pros and cons. Strategic potential versus lack of synergy. Finally potential won out and he pushed the button. "Adam Taylor here."

"Adam, it's Vanessa. How are you?"

"Doing great. Glad to hear from you. How's the weather in L.A.?"

"Fabulous. Listen, I hope you don't mind me calling, but I wanted to get that title that you were recommending."

Title? Geez, what had he said? "Oh, yeah. Listen, I'm in the car. Can I call you from home? Need to check my shelves. I'll get the publisher as well."

I didn't raise you to lie, either.

"Not now, Ma."

"What was that?"

Adam slapped his palm against the steering wheel. "Sorry, Vanessa. Just a little late-afternoon fatigue. I'll call you this evening, okay?"

"Sure. Thanks, Adam." Click.

Nope. Vanessa wasn't it. He'd taken her out once

about three months ago, and although she had the right requirements, the core product seemed off in some way.

He knew what he wanted. A sweet young thing who wanted 2.5 kids and a garden out back. Somebody who understood the concept of home and staying firmly planted in one place.

He had wandered around the country for so long, assignment to assignment, the idea of coming home to one woman, one family sounded like his own personal paradise.

The house had been an impulse buy, a two-story Victorian that he painted when he was back in Alabama.

Now he just needed to find someone to share it with.

An SUV pulled in front of him and he slammed on the brakes. The Porsche slid to a halt and Adam swore under his breath.

"Sorry, Ma. I forgot."

This time the voice in his head didn't reply.

3

AFTER WORK, Jessica always jogged on the path that ran along the lake. Two miles on a normal day and three miles when her thighs got extra dimply, which was usually after having dinner with Cassandra, who liked her desserts.

Today was a good Wednesday. No crisis at the office, the weather was a perfect sixty-five degrees, and the runner in front of her had the most motivating physique she had ever had the sheer pleasure of running after.

Somewhere between mile marker number two and mile marker number three she realized the identity of that motivating physique.

He was right ahead of her. *He* was going to win. She picked up her pace. Not many people could beat her on a quarter-mile sprint, and she prayed Mr. Adam Taylor wasn't one of them.

Time for round two.

Her feet pounded against the caliche track as she found her rhythm. She began to gain on him, noticing the efficient way he moved. Very smooth.

The powerful muscles worked in his legs, and his

back flexed as he ran, making it look easy. His torso was bare, the better to be ogled, my dear.

Jessica stumbled, more caught up in leering than concentrating on the track in front of her. That just made her mad, so she kicked up to the next gear.

"Afternoon, Adam."

He glanced over at her, his eyes taking in her sports bra and shorts. "Afternoon."

"You're pretty good."

"Ditto."

He matched her pace and they ran on in silence, bounded by the skyscrapers of the city and the still waters of Lake Michigan. She concentrated on keeping her breath even and slow.

"How far do you usually go?" he asked, not even winded.

"Five," she answered, sneaking an extra gasp. "You?"

"Five."

"What's your time?" she asked, trying for a casual tone.

His gaze flicked in her direction. "Fifty-five is the usual. I can shave off eight minutes when I'm concentrating. You?"

He had stepped right into her trap. "I can beat that."

"I don't know. I've got a report that I need to turn in before morning."

"Chicken?" She pulled ahead.

"Now you're just talking trash."

She didn't reply except with vaguely unprofessional, yet extremely satisfying, clucking noises.

He pulled alongside her. "That is such a pretty ass. Seems a shame to watch you lose it."

"You think so, farm boy?"

"Oh, yeah."

"Care to bet on that?"

He laughed. "What are we playing for now? I would love to see you in a little, black—"

"No."

"Spoilsport," he said with a heated look that indicated he was still off in fantasyland.

Jessica almost lost her stride. "It's got to be something more meaningful."

"Sex can be meaningful. Great sex can be life-altering."

She snorted in a completely unfeminine manner. "You are such a man. Loser buys dinner."

"Cooks, not buys."

"And a chauvinist, too. I bet you can't cook."

"You can't even begin to imagine."

"You're just trying to get me alone."

He clutched a hand to his extremely well-formed, sweat-glistened chest. "Gee, she sees right through me."

"Buys dinner. Public place. Ready?" She shot forward before he could reply. "See you at the finish line."

They kept even for three miles, but the fast pace started to get to Jessica. He didn't look winded at all, chest pumping in even rhythm. Was he slowing his pace just to let her win?

That demeaning thought got her through another one and a half miles. By the time they reached the last half-mile marker, Jessica thought her heart was going to explode. Still she ran, concentrating on putting one foot forward. Finding the zone.

Adam started to pull ahead. Two lengths, then three.

No way.

She blocked out everything. This was the man who thought he could beat her. Had already beaten her once. Not again in this lifetime. She focused on nothing but his black silk running shorts covering his mighty fine—

Stop it, Jessica. Her pace picked up.

The final marker loomed ahead, the shadowy clump of trees and the water fountain that sparkled like a desert oasis. Almost there.

She fell in beside him.

He pulled ahead.

No.

Not just no, but *hell no.*

Adam took the lead.

He smiled at her, slow and sure. A victory smile.

Calling on every ounce of her reserves, she shot forward, leaving him behind.

He almost caught her, but she was determined.

There it was.

One more length.

She felt his breath hot on her back. Still she ran.

There.

There.

She zoomed past the marker, two strides ahead of Mr. Hotshot. "There."

He came to a stop next to her, and she was grateful to see his bare chest pumping wildly, the sweat dribbling down between sharply-defined pecs. "You *are* good," he murmured, almost to himself.

Jessica forced herself to look away.

"In all things, Taylor." She leaned against the tree, sucking much-needed air into her starving lungs. The world spun four times before it righted itself once more. She swept a hand through her hair, wiping the sweat off her forehead.

His thumb brushed against her lower lip. "You missed a spot."

Her lashes drifted down, and she fought the urge to taste him. A frightening thought. Instantly the warm touch was gone and she stepped back into reality. "You owe me dinner."

"You beat me, Barnes. I'll pick you up tomorrow night at eight."

For a second he sounded pleased, as if he had planned the whole thing. Suspicion tainted the moment. She stood, hands on hips, and studied his face. He looked exhausted and tousled, in a "hey baby, come jump me" kind of way. Once again, she felt the taste of victory. And it was sweet. The suspicion was gone. "717 West Patterson, apartment 2285. Think you can remember that, Taylor?"

"Don't underestimate me, Barnes. I'll see you tomorrow."

JESSICA PUT her key in the lock to 87 Spruce Avenue, turned the latch and pushed inside. *Home.* Her mom shouted a greeting from the kitchen, followed by the familiar rapid-fire barrage of requests. Set the table, chase the cat from the back bedroom and bring the clean laundry up from the basement. Jessica breathed in the ever-present aroma of fabric softener and cinnamon. Yup. Definitely home.

The family homestead in the southwest side of the city had been built proudly in 1937 by her grandfather, Elijah Barnes. An extra bathroom had been added on when Jessica was born, the attic had been finished when her brother Patrick turned seven, and four years ago her father had added a one-car garage to keep the snow off the 1987 Buick. For Jessica, it was the only home she'd ever known.

After carrying out her orders, Jessica made her way into the kitchen where her mother whisked from stove to sink to counter and back, faster than the eye could follow. There was never a wasted movement; she never stopped the way Jessica did, wondering what it was she intended to do.

Diane Barnes was a woman who kept a spotless house, was happiest when her children were nearby and had never met a casserole she didn't like. From an early age, Jessica had known she was not her mother's daughter. When Jessica had lived at home, they had fought almost every day. Her mom didn't understand a career woman, and Jessica believed housework was one of the original eight plagues of Egypt, but because the Bible had been written by a man, it never got included.

Jessica watched her mother for a moment, then felt guilty and began putting things away, simply so she could look busy. "How you doing, Mom?"

Her mother lifted a lid from the pot on the stove, stirring idly. "Same as always, Jess."

"You should take it easy some. You look tired," Jessica said, noting the way her mother's skin looked more fragile than usual.

Diane shook her head in a patient manner, her short brown hair rippling with movement. "I've got too many things to do, and the days are only getting shorter," she answered, setting a stack of plates in Jessica's hands.

Obediently, Jessica trotted out to the dining table and laid out the plates, moving from place to place until the spoons were lined up exactly parallel with the napkins and the forks gleamed in the bright lights from the wall sconces that were fixed around the room.

The dining table had already been set up for Wednesday dinner, five settings. It was family night at the Barnes household. Her father, Frank Barnes, had the chair at the head of the table, but until the food was actually on his plate, he sat in his recliner watching the news, thinking of new names for the local aldermen.

Jessica poked her head into the den. "Pop, supper is almost ready," she yelled.

From behind the back of his brown easy chair came a grunt of acknowledgment. It usually took a good three tries to get Pop to leave the chair, which was incredibly inefficient, but you couldn't skip one or he wouldn't leave. Jessica sighed.

The front door slammed, rattling the bay window in a precarious manner. Patrick was home.

At the ripe old age of eighteen, Patrick had moved out of the house and set out on his own. For two years he'd skipped Wednesday dinners, but about the time he turned twenty, White Castle burgers had lost some of their appeal and he'd developed an appreciation for a home-cooked meal. He was now twenty-five and thought he knew everything. Jessica knew better.

He took off his jacket and threw it on top of the coat tree in the hall. "Hey, Jess. Can you get me something to drink?"

"You been taking drugs, Patrick? Do I look like Mom?"

"More and more every day," he said, pausing before he walked into the den to pinch her cheek.

Jessica smacked her fist into her palm. "I'm your older sister, I'm the professional in the family."

"Blah, blah, blah."

The front door slammed again. Not quite as loudly

as Patrick, which meant that Ian was now home from class. He was shorter than Jessica by a couple of inches, but what he lacked in height, he said he made up for in wisdom.

He flung his jacket on the coat tree and shook his head. "Sis, you always let him get to you. The only reason he does that is to get you mad."

It was the ultimate humiliation to get behavioral lessons from her baby brother. At least he was the scholar as well, which soothed her ego somewhat. Ian had spent three years in the local community college, trying out different majors to see if they suited him. Eventually he'd wandered full circle back to Business Administration and had just been accepted to Notre Dame.

Ian threw his backpack onto the sideboard in the dining room, but then their mother scuttled into the room and moved it into the hall closet, with nary a word of complaint. Jessica couldn't believe her brother's inconsiderate nature. "Would it have been so much trouble to put it away yourself? Don't you think Mom has enough to do without having to pick up after you?"

"Heavy stress at the job, Jess?"

She glared at Ian and then she sneezed. "You couldn't imagine."

"Yeah, I can." He rubbed his hands together, his eyes gleaming with possibilities. "I can't wait."

He looked so excited, so full of enthusiasm, and Jessica didn't have the heart to enlighten him about the real state of affairs in the business world. Maybe she was turning into a cynic. More likely she was just scared.

Her mother called from the kitchen. "Jessica, would you find out what everyone would like to drink, please?"

"Sure, Mom," she said, collecting drink orders and pondering a career in the field of hotel and restaurant management. By the time she had returned to her mother with the information, she had decided that the hospitality industry might be a possibility. And of course, she'd forgotten what everyone wanted to drink.

Ten minutes later they were all seated at the table, and her father said grace, the same blessing he'd said for all twenty-nine years of Jessica's life. Short, to the point and sincere. Not fancy, but it was the Barnes way.

Dinner was never a quiet affair, although Jessica wondered what it was like Thursday through Tuesday when it was just her mother and father. Did they talk about the day or get silly, or was it just like tonight with her father buried in the news and her mother buried in the kitchen?

The menu tonight was roast beef, gravy, Jessica's favorite green-bean casserole and homemade rolls. It made Jessica weak just thinking of cooking all that stuff day after day, night after night. She watched her mother fuss over everyone with appreciation and more than a little concern.

Diane held up the rose-colored gravy boat. "More gravy, Ian? And don't forget your vegetables."

Her father took a bite of roast beef and emitted a long "ahhh" of satisfaction. "Those guys in meat-packing can tell me what they want, but there's nothing closer to heaven than your roast beef, Diane."

Her mother glowed and picked at her plate. "Thank you, Frank."

That was all her father had to say? Jessica went to the sideboard and refilled her mother's water glass.

"That's all well and good, but shouldn't Mom have a night off every now and then?"

Her father shoveled a bit of roast beef into his mouth.

Jessica shot Ian a plea for moral support, but he was too much of a pacifist or a chicken—or both—to assist.

It was a battle she would have to fight alone. "Mom deserves to get some rest. You got a birthday coming up, don't you, Mom?"

Her mother got up and spooned more green beans onto Ian's plate. "In June."

Immediately Jessica knew how to solve this problem. "I think we should have a party."

"Oh, I don't know, Jessica."

So typical. If no one leaped to her mom's defense, she'd never get a break. Well, Jessica wasn't about to let her back out now. She locked eyes with her mom. "No, no, wait. Hear me out. I don't want you to worry about cooking or cleaning or being a hostess. I'll take care of everything. The party will be my birthday present for you. And we can get your hair cut at one of those chi-chi places in the Loop. And your nails. You gotta get your nails done."

Her mother still didn't look convinced. "I suppose it could be fun."

Jessica stood and paced around the table, continuing in full marketing, project-planning mode. It helped to have something to take her mind off the job issues right now and finally she had a chance to give something back to her mother. "We'll have your friends and your side of the family..."

Alarmed, her father looked up. "You're not inviting Aunt Alys. The woman eats enough for ten. Jessica, you'll go broke just trying to feed her."

Diane waved a hand at her husband. "Hush, Frank."

"There's nothing wrong with a healthy appetite," Jessica piped in.

"And I wouldn't dare not invite her," her mother added.

Frank rubbed a hand over the remaining twirls of dark hair that covered his scalp. "Oy. She's coming, then? Jessica, I'm hoping that job of yours pays well, 'cause you're going to have a hell of a bill."

"I'm doing fine."

"My little girl is going be vice president someday, I know it." Her father grinned, his dark eyes glowing, and Jessica felt a little kick in her heart.

"You bet I will," Jessica promised, ignoring the twinge in her stomach that seemed to indicate otherwise.

ADAM SHOWED UP at her door at eight o'clock sharp on Thursday. Much to his delight, Jessica greeted him at the door with a prickly smile and a wisp of a dress. All the blood drained from his head and he experienced a twenty-percent loss in mental capacity.

It was good. That much he knew. Sparkling, the material moved around her like liquid gold. The front was two strips of cloth that clung to her breasts. How? He didn't know, but he was happy.

She smiled at his obvious discomfort. "Problem, Taylor?"

Her voice was smooth and confident. This was a woman who liked her power. Her idea of home was behind a desk. High risk, low return. Remember that, he told himself. He held out a hand. "Not at all."

He made the requisite small talk as they made their way to his car. Then he flicked the keyless entry and opened the passenger door.

Adam had learned to expect a myriad of reactions to his car. Fascination and awe, and a few dates had turned—well, insatiable. And who was he to complain? But there was no awe in Jessica's expression now, no sexual hunger, darn it, just—anger? This was a new one.

"Is there a problem?" he asked, still holding open the door. Maybe that was a mistake? Maybe she didn't like the man-opening-car-door protocol. Well, damned if he was going to lose his manners for her.

"You drive a Porsche."

"Yes," he answered.

"A 911 Carrera Coupe." She splayed a hand over the roof, her fingers smoothing over it like a lover's caress. "It's lapis blue, isn't it?"

He nodded, now completely fascinated. His consultant's training told him to hold his tongue.

"A 3.6-liter engine, 320 horsepower?"

Except when a woman started talking horsepower. "Zero to sixty in under five seconds."

Her hand dropped to her side and she sneezed. "You're an evil man, Taylor."

Perhaps if he hadn't tallied the final head-count projections today he would have been more receptive, but the insult hit close to home. His voice rose a notch, just one, before he got control. "Because I drive a Porsche?"

She jabbed the hood with an energetic finger. "That's my car."

Adam ran a hand through his hair, muddling his way through. "Did someone steal your car?"

She shook her head and sneezed again. "No. I don't own the car. It's my goal."

Adam reached in his pocket and took out the travel package of tissues he'd brought just for her. "Here."

Obediently she blew her nose, wadded the paper in her hand, and then faced him, liquid gold in the bright lights of the street. "I'm sorry. It's a long story and very silly, and I won't bore you with the details. Can I just say that I'm a little overwrought and we can leave it at that?''

Overwrought, my butt. He thought about pressing her for the truth, but the night was young. She glanced toward the car, more longing in her eyes than he really wanted to see wasted on a Porsche. Inspiration struck and he held out his keys. ''Why don't you drive?''

She palmed the keys, lightly stroking the metal. He watched in silence, wondered at the oddly vulnerable expression on her face. And then it was gone.

She threw the keys in the air, caught them with one hand and was settled in the driver's side before he could open the door. Damn. He walked around, opened it, shut it. ''Just making sure it's closed,'' and then folded his legs in the passenger side.

''You know how to drive a stick, Barnes?''

''Just watch me.''

And the car roared into the night.

THE RESTAURANT was cool and chic. Not like the normal places that Jessica chose to spend her dining dollars, but she couldn't help the cocky swing in her hips when she crossed the elegant threshold.

Jessica Barnes had arrived, holding tight to the strong arm of Adam Taylor. Okay, technically he was still the enemy, but for tonight—tonight he was her dream man.

He was her imaginary date to the prom, the football player that had never asked her out. He was the Saturday-night phone call that never came. All neatly packaged into one living, breathing, sexy-as-hell man.

And by the way, did she forget to mention that he drove a very cool car?

Her sigh of pleasure was long overdue. Eleven years of doubts pent up inside her. It felt good to let it all out.

After they were seated and had gotten their drinks, she sipped her wine like a pro. He took off his jacket and she studied the way his tanned skin balanced the stark white of his shirt. Nice. She liked the way his gaze lingered on her, appreciation in those gray-green eyes, desire there as well.

She leaned forward, tempting the fates. "How did you become a consultant?"

"You don't want to know."

"Yes, I really do."

"Fresh out of school with an MBA, there weren't that many jobs. I took the first offer I got, a position at one of the big consulting houses. That lasted for about three years, about the time I discovered I was good at operational efficiency." He stared off into the distance, tugging at his tie.

"A rare talent," she murmured.

He turned back to her and shrugged. "It's what I do. How about you? You like numbers, huh?"

"I've always liked math, and finance seemed the way to go. I found Hard-Wire about two years after I graduated." She remembered the day she'd told her parents her plans for VP. She would even spring for champagne. A vice president had never set foot in the Barnes household before and she was determined to rectify that little situation.

He watched her from over his glass. "Are you from Chicago?"

"Born and raised. And you? You've got this accent. What's with it?"

"Alabama."

"No kidding? A.L.? You don't look like what I imagined a guy from the twenty-second state would be like."

"A.L.?" He laughed. "So what am I supposed to look like?"

"You know, overalls, a piece of hay clamped between your teeth, rural. You look urban. You clean up good, Mr. Taylor."

"Thank ye kindly, ma'am."

It felt comfortable to sit here with him: talking, laughing. Trusting him. A shiver ran down her spine. That was a bad thing. "Let's not overdo it."

His smile faded, the mood broken.

"How's the report coming?" she asked, making sure she didn't forget.

All traces of a smile disappeared completely. "Let's not go there tonight, hmm? I don't want to talk about work, I'm more interested in you."

"I'm boring."

His eyes met hers and he shook his head slowly. "I don't think so. Got any secrets, Jessica?"

"I ran away from home when I was sixteen. Was

gone about seven hours before I came back. Mom and Pop still don't know. Does that count?"

"Why'd you run away?"

"Life sucks for everybody at sixteen. I wasn't any different." It had been Black Tuesday. She'd been passed over for the drill team, after already having been passed over for cheerleader, after already losing the class council race. It was a bad year. She sneezed, reached for a tissue, and when she was done, immediately lost it under the table. "You? What were you like at sixteen?"

"Hauling hay, plowing the fields, helping Ma when I could." As he talked his accent got deeper, running through her like a slow shot of Southern Comfort.

"What about your father?"

"He was always gone. Assignment here, assignment there."

"But your mother still wanted the farm?"

"It was her home." There was a contented smile on his face, a plowboy from Alabama. She had teased him about it, but never actually believed she was right.

The waiter interrupted, announcing the night's specials, but Jessica ignored him. It was Adam that intrigued her. She understood him a little better, understood why he was as driven as she was. A man who wanted a new start in a new place.

Adam took the menu from the table and glanced over it. Completely casual at first. She didn't get wise to him until he angled it in the direction of the door.

"Dodging someone, Taylor? You got any secrets of your own?"

The menu didn't move. "It's not a secret. It was—*she* was a date."

A date. Why was she surprised? She kept her voice light, kept the disappointment close inside. "And the plot thickens. What sort of date? Did you promise to call her, but never did? Or even worse, were you supposed to see her tonight? For shame, Mr. Taylor. For shame."

The menu lowered and he rubbed his eyes. "I have a conscience. I don't need two. It's just not good business practice to exchange social pleasantries with one date when I'm out on another."

Oh.

And up to the table walked a woman who caught the eye of every man in the room—the sort of woman who knew nitric acid and had experienced it daily. "Adam? Is that you?"

Jessica fought jealousy, fought a sneeze. Instead, she settled for a smug "Busted" that she made sure he could hear.

Adam shot her a dirty look, and then instantly flashed his consultant's smile at the blonde leaning oh-so-elegantly against the table. "Hello, Fallon."

Fallon? Jessica mouthed the name to Adam. The sneak ignored her.

"How are you doing, Adam? I've been waiting for the book club to meet again so I could get your take on *Sula*. Have you finished it yet?"

Book club? Okay, he was definitely not a man but an alien life form raised on the farm land of Alabama, and now assuming the guise of a consultant. The truth was out there after all.

The subject of her conspiracy theory looked very uncomfortable.

Jessica balanced her chin on her hand, awaiting his answer.

"Not yet. I haven't been able to focus my energies on the story and a book isn't any good unless you approach it with the proper frame of reference." At long last, Adam remembered his manners. "Fallon, this is Jessica Barnes. Jessica, Fallon Morningside."

Jessica held out a hand. "Pleased to meet you, Miss Morningside."

"Oh, it's just Fallon. I hear Miss Morningside all day, every day. It gets old."

Jessica forced a bright smile on her face. "What do you do?"

"I teach special needs children in Bridgeport. What do you do, Jessica?" The tall blonde exuded grace, charm and, worst of all, she seemed nice. Jessica felt a telltale tickle in her nose. Not now. Please not now.

"I'm in finance." It sounded so trivial, so meaningless, and in three short seconds she realized her entire life's ambition had just been one-upped by a schoolteacher.

She fumbled for a tissue and came up empty. Not now. A napkin. She just needed to get to the napkin.

No. It was too late. She turned her head away from the table. *Ha-choo.*

"God bless you." Fallon's wonderfully melodic tones winged their way through the air.

Jessica shot upright and mumbled, "Thanks."

"I'll let the two of you enjoy your dinner. I highly recommend the chateaubriand. They cook it perfectly. Adam, I'll see you on Tuesday." She wiggled a couple of fingers in his direction, yet somehow it didn't look goofy. On Jessica it would be goofy.

Jessica sighed and felt another sneeze coming on.

Adam studied the menu with intense fascination.

Jessica studied Adam. "She's nice."

"Yes. The salmon sounds really good. What are you going to have?"

She played with the silverware, tapping the fork over the knife. "I did some volunteer work when I was in high school. It wasn't special needs kids or anything, but they were poor."

"The lobster looks good, too. Don't you think?"

Not quite satisfied, she tapped the fork a little harder. "I give to the United Way, you know."

"Jessica." Adam took away her fork and then patted her hand. "Let it go. You're a fine human being."

"Thank you," she answered. Suddenly her lifelong goal of a Porsche seemed petty, but the car maneuvered so well.

She glanced across the table and decided it was time to forget about her shortcomings. That would come later. For now she wanted to enjoy the evening.

"What are you going to have?" he asked again.

"Oh. Food." She looked over the menu. "I'll have the linguini with clam sauce, I think."

They ordered and Adam stayed quiet. Thinking about Fallon, probably. Jessica could nip that in the bud. "She seems nice."

"Who?"

"Fallon. You met her at a book club?"

"Yes."

"A book club?"

"Yes." This time he sounded defensive, and he tugged at his tie.

She took a long sip of wine, until her loins were fully girded, and then asked the question that she really wanted answered. "And just how many men are in this book club?"

"Me."

"And you really read all the books? It's not just a way to meet women?"

His smile grew wider. "Do you really think I'm twisted enough to join a book club just to meet women?"

Calculating the possibility, she ran her tongue over her teeth. "Absolutely," was her final answer.

"You're slaying me here, Barnes."

"Do you have book clubs in every city you work in?"

He shrugged. "Not all of them."

The waiter brought their salads, effectively ending the conversation.

For the moment.

She changed the topic of conversation and they argued baseball. She liked the Cubs, he liked the Yankees. They argued late-night talk shows. He liked Letterman, she liked Leno. They argued hardware. He thought switches would become obsolete, she thought he was full of it.

Eventually, the waiter arrived with the entrées, and they ate their dinners in silence. Every now and then their gazes would collide and Jessica felt the warm flush prickle her skin.

At last the table was cleared and the bill paid. "You like to dance?" he asked. "There's a club down the street."

She knew what dancing would involve, a loud band, smoke and probably very little touching. "No thanks."

"Then I'll just take you home," he said, his voice low, full of promise. Promises that involved touching.

She struggled to breathe, images of touching playing in her head. "Home," she echoed.

Adam drove this time, the hum of the car's engine a contented purr that suited her mood nicely. When they reached the garage, she started to wish she'd cleaned up her apartment a little more, that she had shopped for better lingerie. Something sexy. Did she have anything sexy? There was an old teddy, but it had got washed in hot water and had never recovered.

Was she going to have sex?

Sex. Oh my God. Panic started in her throat and worked its way down between her thighs.

"Jess." A hand touched her shoulder, a whisper-touch and she jumped.

"You okay?"

She noticed the emptiness of the parking garage, the intent look on his face. The seat belts came off. Her smile was simply because it felt right, because he felt right.

He leaned over her and his hand cupped her jaw. She leaned into his strength, relishing the feeling of protection. Her mind slowed, the warning in her head pushed away by her own recklessness. Tomorrow she would worry. Tonight, to the moon.

His fingers slid beneath her chin, tilting her face until their gazes were locked together. His eyes were shadowed in darkness, but it didn't take a mind reader to understand his message.

Then his lips closed over hers and all other thoughts floated away.

The first touch was gentle, a soft brushing of lips, as if both were afraid of the fire. Her heart beat twice before the fire burned, the gentleness gone. His fingers tightened on her jaw, and his tongue swept into her mouth. It was no request, only a demand. She heard a gasp. Her own.

Jessica curled her hands into his hair, tangling her fingers in the dark silk.

The scent of leather clouded in the air, mingling with the sharp musk of his cologne. His hands held her firm. At first, his mouth was slow, seductive, his tongue teasing her with an insidious rhythm.

She struggled to move close, angle her hips against his, but she discovered the sharp constraints of bucket seats. Damned car.

But then he had his hands on her and she forgot all her complaints. His fingers dipped low in her dress, finding a hard nipple on the first try. The thin material was no obstacle to him and he pulled it aside, his thumbs brushing against her breasts.

Slow, oh geez, it was too slow. Her breasts rose to meet his touch, needing more from him.

With one low moan, his kiss turned hard, taking what he pleased, and Jessica held on tight for the ride. Never in her life had a man ravaged her mouth, but there was a hunger in him that she wouldn't dream of denying. An ache between her thighs pulsed, just as firmly as her heart.

The games were forgotten, everything was forgotten except her need for him.

HE HAD TO STOP THIS or he was going to go insane. He had spent his whole life polishing an image, but now his image was blowing up in his face. This wasn't right.

Her legs shifted restlessly, trying to pull him closer to her, trying to fit him against her. She was like an armful of flame, and he needed to find the strength to resist. For God's sake—they were in a car.

It was no small feat to end the kiss, and he was

mighty proud when he did. His eyes locked with hers, a muscle ticking in his jaw. "I need to leave. Now. I'll walk you up."

Her mouth opened then closed, her lips still swollen from his kiss. Her eyes had lost the soft haze they'd worn earlier. Now they were hard. He knew the exact moment when she remembered who he was.

She adjusted her dress with a shaking hand, but he didn't dare touch her. If he did, he wouldn't have stopped.

They made it out of the car without saying a word, her heels echoing a smart clip on the concrete pavement, and they walked to the elevator. Opposite sides for three floors.

He was going to explain this to her. Explain that making love was a bad idea. Explain to her that he was going home to settle in Alabama when this whole damned assignment was done.

But she never looked at him once.

When they got to her door, she fumbled with the keys and he reached out to help her. Finally the damned thing was open, and she turned to face him.

"Sorry, Taylor. Don't know what's come over me." She braced one arm against the door, a casual gesture.

"Jess." He reached out to touch her, and she jerked away.

Damn.

He tried to straighten the mess he'd made. If he had just kept to his normal business procedures, none of this would have happened. "Don't be mad. This isn't right. It wouldn't be fair to you."

She closed her eyes, and he wanted to help, to touch her, but he didn't dare. "We can't see each other," she said.

It was nothing less than he should have expected, but what was so unexpected was how much it hurt. "That could be a problem. We see each other every day."

"So we keep things on the level. Strictly business. How hard can that be?" she said, and then started to laugh without any humor.

Adam was a consultant, a professional arbitrator. When there was a compromise to be found, he was there. "How about a cooling-off period? Ten days," he said, simply because he couldn't go longer without touching her again.

She thrust a hand through her hair, and he remembered how the silky strands had felt between his fingers. "That sounds so cold. How could you just switch it off like that?"

"I don't. I just have to keep away from you."

"All right. Ten days. It's a bet."

"What do you mean?" he asked.

"Ten days. Trust me, it'll be easier if I turn it into a bet."

It sounded like such a bad idea, but he knew what she was doing. It was the perfect way to keep Jessica Barnes at a distance. Threaten her with the one thing she couldn't bear—defeat. "We're going to do this, aren't we?" he asked in a tired voice, ready to bend to the inevitable, ready to do anything to avoid hurting her.

Already the wheels were turning in her head, plotting new ways to win. "Let's just be clear about the ground rules," she said, her voice picking up steam.

There weren't supposed to be rules. "No rules."

"There's always rules. Ten days. Full penetration."

His mouth went dry. "Pardon?"

"Foreplay—which you're very good at, by the way—doesn't count."

He forgot his lines. "I think foreplay should count. This is supposed to be a cooling-off period," he said, trying to remember why he wanted a cooling-off period."

"I can take it," she said, so resolutely he wanted to disagree simply on principle.

He was toast. Stay the course, Taylor, remember the purpose. "Ten days from today or ten days from tomorrow?"

"I'll give you a handicap. Ten days from tomorrow." He loved to hear the snap of smug confidence back in her voice. They were doing the right thing after all.

He turned to leave, turned to go home to a long cold shower. Ten days. How hard could it be?

He'd almost made it to the elevator.

"Adam, what are the stakes?" she called down the hall.

He hadn't made it out of the fog of thoughts of foreplay yet. "The stakes?"

"You know, what are we betting on?"

He ran a hand through his hair and clutched his keys like the lifeline they weren't. "Whatever the winner wants."

She leaned against the door frame, long legs crossed in front of her. "Anything goes?" Long legs and a saucy mouth.

He punched the elevator button. Down. Hard. "Anything goes," he whispered to himself. Oh, hell.

4

MICKEY LOOKED UP from her glass of beer. "I thought you had a hot date."

Jessica fell into the brown leather bar chair. "I did."

"You're home way too early for a good date. Sorry, Jess," Cassandra said, all the while making eyes at the bartender. He was new—and a little young on Jessica's age barometer—but she didn't like to judge.

Besides, tonight she felt pumped. Even for an early night, it was one of the best dates she'd had in a long time. Resist Adam Taylor? Not a problem. Of course, she could still taste his kiss. She took a long sip of Cassandra's beer. Better, but it was still there, the sizzle just at the edge of her lips.

"Hey!"

"Sorry, I was thirsty." Jessica smiled smugly at Cassandra. It wasn't very often that she was the one out on the date, and Cassandra was the one belly-up to the bar. "It was a good date, a great date."

"And who was the mystery man?" Cassandra asked, one perfectly groomed eyebrow lifting elegantly.

Jessica stared at the three inquisitive faces, and knew a moment of panic. She wasn't ready to admit that she'd gone out with the enemy. An enemy with wayward hands and a mouth that kissed like in the movies. "Uh, just a guy I met on the train."

Mickey shook her head. "Jessica, you can't just go picking up strange men and then let them pick you up at your apartment. You could get abducted or dismembered or have parts of you whacked off."

"We really shouldn't let you watch the news, Mick. I drove," Jessica replied, not quite a lie.

"Oh, well, that's okay then. So, are you going to see him again?" Beth asked, her chin in her palm, her eyes big in her small face.

"Maybe."

Mickey didn't say a word, just looked at Jessica with that "I'm-not-buying-a-word-of-this" look. They'd talk later.

"Where'd you go eat? Steaks, continental? Oh, I love that new place on St. Clair. They have a lobster risotto to die for. Twenty-five points, but you know, I'd starve myself for three days to stay on track."

Sometimes Beth was really amazing, and Jessica gawked with suitable appreciation. "How do you know the point values from a restaurant?"

"Got an inside line with the chef. He's my brother's wife's plumber."

Mickey pursed her lips thoughtfully, considering what they all were. "And he's a chef?"

"Yeah."

She pushed her beer aside. This *was* serious. "You should marry him, Beth."

Slowly Beth shook her head. "Can't. He doesn't play on my side of the fence, if you know what I mean. Not that there's anything wrong with that, but you'd think they'd realize what they're missing."

Jess sighed. So that was the way of it. All the good ones were gay or divorced. Or ax-men. "It's a cold, cruel world out there," she said, all the while wondering if Adam Taylor could fix lobster risotto or broken pipes.

"I got a new job," Beth stated, and that brought them all to attention. Beth wasn't quite responsible enough for a job, and after Kenny had left, she'd moved from one thing to another.

"You're kidding? Where?"

"Starbucks."

"You're making coffee for a living?" asked Cassandra, who had been known to frequent Starbucks on occasion.

"Yeah, for now. I need to get back on my own two feet."

Jessica didn't mention that Beth had never truly been on one of her own feet, much less two. "That's great," she said. "Now we can go harass you at work."

Beth stood and pushed her chair back. "Well, gotta go, have to open up at four-thirty."

"*A.m.?*" Cassandra asked, as close to screeching as she got. She was a professional diamond cutter, third generation for the Ward family, and never showed up before ten.

"Yeah, it's early. But it's something I've got to do."

For others it was climbing Everest. For Beth, it was getting her new job.

"Knock 'em dead, tiger."

Beth sauntered off, for the first time a confidence in her walk. "I will."

"Excuse me, girls. My dream man awaits," said Cassandra, off to schmooze with a banker-type sitting on the far side of the bar.

"You think she's gone for the night?"

Jessica studied the intended victim and nodded. "Oh, yeah. He's got drool on his lips already. It takes at least a day before she gets bored with the little guppies and throws them back in the water."

"She's got a four-carat diamond where her heart should be," Mickey replied.

"Blame Benedict O'Malley," said Jessica, thinking that the world would have been a better place if he could've just left Cassandra alone.

"I don't know if he can take all the blame. Some of it must be genetic. Those Wards were always a weird bunch. Who knows what's really in their DNA?"

Having met the Ward family once or twice, Jessica was inclined to agree, but her own relations didn't put her in a position to cast stones.

When she thought of her family, it made her think of job security, job security made her think of Adam—in the bad way, not the chair-squirming way, and she wasn't ready to think of the bad way again—so she shrugged it off and concentrated on another issue.

"Maybe. Speaking of families, I need your help. I have to plan a birthday party for Mom."

"She actually asked you to do that?"

"It's her fiftieth. I decided for once, instead of cooking for the entire Barnes clan, she should have the work done for her."

"You? Cook? You have no kitchen. Have you forgotten that important fact?"

"*Au contraire.* Catering, baby—that's my motto."

"Talk to Beth. Food is her specialty."

"She took off before I could broach the subject. Need to find a band, too."

"What are you looking for? Swing? Jazz?"

Jessica couldn't remember the last time she'd seen her mom dance, she wanted the party to be one her mother would never forget. Something fabulous. Classy. Sophisticated. "Maybe a string quartet?"

Mickey's dark brows drew down into a V behind her glasses, but she didn't say a word. Instead, she sipped her beer and then jumped right in with both feet. "Date with Adam?"

And Jessica didn't even try to lie. "How'd you know?"

"You're emitting radioactive pheromones and no telltale sneezing."

It was a sad state of affairs that her nose banned her from having secrets. "Very funny."

"I wasn't being funny."

Jessica buried her face in her hands. "I know. Don't say anything."

"Seeing him again, huh?"

"Don't know." Jessica looked up into Mickey's piercing blue eyes, debating what to tell, what not to, but secrets weren't exactly her forte, and Mick was her best friend. "We have a bet."

The least Mickey could have done was to look surprised—a polite widening of the eyes, a simple exclamation, but of course she didn't. "What'd you bet on now?"

Jessica sighed. "He bet I couldn't resist him. Ten days. I have to hold out for ten days."

Mickey considered that for a minute. "Ten days? You can handle that. Hell, Cassandra could handle that."

"Of course I can," Jessica answered and took another sip of Mickey's beer. "Ten days will be a snap." And then, to prove her point, she tried to snap her fingers together. But all she could do was sneeze.

THE NEXT MORNING, the Stevenson Expressway was bumper to bumper. A truck had dumped some sort of noxious toxin all over the place, and two lanes were closed. It was a pisser of a way to start the day, sitting in his car, watching the asphalt trucks fill the potholes.

Adam turned down the volume on the CD player. Somehow he didn't feel like listening to Kenny Wayne today. Instead he felt like an ass.

And so you should, his conscience answered back.

"I suppose a man can't castigate himself in peace.

Of course his mother must join in. Don't they keep you busy up there?''

Don't try and distract me with that small talk. I think you're going to take advantage of her, then practice your so-long speech, and then—as if that isn't enough—arrange for a pink slip as well.

"It's called voluntary separation program. Compensation packages are attractive and full of perks. The term *pink slip* is passé and poor for morale, as well."

His conscience was suspiciously quiet.

"I'm not going to sleep with her. She's not going to come near me because of the bet." But still he worried. He had seen the gleam in her eye. A gleam he thought might have been reflected in his own.

She's a nice girl.

Adam jabbed a finger at the stereo and cranked up the volume. "I can't hear you."

She's got great taste in cars.

That made him turn the volume down. "You know, I knew you were going to say something about that. All it means is that she's as status-conscious as you are."

Hush your mouth.

"Oh come on, Ma. Why did you want a Porsche, huh? Because you liked the way the engine sounded? Nooo. It was to impress all the old busybodies when you zipped down the streets of Fort Payne." Now it was his conscience arguing. He had promised his mom she would have a Porsche, but he'd been a little too late.

I would do no such thing. 'Cepting maybe on Sunday afternoons after church.

Adam's phone rang and he thanked God for the interruption. "Taylor."

"Mr. Taylor, Barnes & Noble, State Street. This is Emily. Your books are in."

"Books?" *Had he ordered books?*

"Yes, Patterson and Clancy."

The new Patterson? Finally. "I'll be by in the next few days to pick them up. Thanks for your help, Emily."

"Anytime, Mr. Taylor. We like to go the extra mile to make sure our customers have something to read. Did you know that Cussler has a new Dirk Pitt title coming out in two weeks? Can I put you on the list?"

"Sure, thanks."

Adam hung up the phone and cranked up the volume on his stereo once more. But the sounds didn't ease his conscience. God, he hated it when his mother was right. He had to make sure Jessica—44713—stayed away from him. All he had to do was to make sure that she saw the real Adam Taylor. The smooth-as-glass consultant who wouldn't know conviction if it bit him in the ass. He just needed to stay on task and let his normal, shlocky mentality shine. Because if she really knew him, she'd never come near him again.

At 9:40 a.m., Adam straightened his tie, picked up his notes, and headed for the 10:00 a.m. financial meeting.

A little early, but he hadn't seen Jessica yet this morning, and her office blinds remained stubbornly closed.

He knew she'd be there, waiting in the fishbowl conference room, calculator in hand. As it was, he shouldn't be excited about seeing her. He should be practicing his lines and planning the destruction of any sexy thoughts she might have about the two of them. All-out, full annihilation to any ideas of ever seeing Jessica wearing nothing more than the golden luster of skin. Liquidating all those images of that mouth pressing against his flesh. Death to those ideas of full penetration.

Oh, God. Now he'd gone and reached critical mass.

He closed his eyes and sank into his chair, contemplating full penetration for just one glorious minute. One moment turned into ten, then fifteen. This couldn't go on.

He stood up, realigned the fundamental feedback in his pants, and tried to focus on something else. Like the report, for instance. At least for now it seemed to help and he headed for the conference room.

As he worked his way through the maze of boxes and chairs that lined the hallways, the floor hummed with activity. Hard-Wire was expanding their borders within the fourteenth-floor office space they used and the sounds of hammers and drills filled the confines.

He stopped to let a workman pass by in the narrow pathway, and listened as a secretary explained patiently into the phone that no, they didn't sell nails here. Now that was something he hadn't considered before. When Hard-Wire became the next company under the confines of the JCN umbrella, the product name would have to be changed.

Then he turned the corner and saw her. Today, she was wearing pants and a jacket that just matched the soft brown of her hair. And sure enough, there was the trusty calculator and folder in hand. Jessica hadn't spied him yet, so he took a moment to absorb the mild shock wave he felt every time he was in her presence.

"You're early," Adam said, starting on the offensive, as if he wasn't early, too.

She gestured toward the pack of papers in her hand. "I needed to go over some things."

Somewhere in the distance a box fell, and he dodged a passing workman in blue. Why was she out here in the war zone? He gestured to the open doorway. "Why don't you go on in?"

"Abercrombie's in there eating an early lunch. It's not pretty."

"Who's Abercrombie?"

"Mail room."

"Break room is full?" he asked, raising his voice to be heard over the hammering.

"They moved the new Q&A contractor in there temporarily. When the space is complete, the lunch room will be free." She leaned back against the wall, looking comfortable in his presence. Number 44713 looked entirely too comfortable.

Adam shook his head. He needed to stick to the agenda. Smarmy and cosmopolitan. Best practices for the guy who needs to strike out. "So. I had some trouble sleeping last night. Hot dreams."

Her mouth fell open, and suddenly he was just one of ten thousand guys with a bad pickup line. "I beg your pardon?" she said.

He put his arm against the wall, mere inches from her hair. He almost touched it, but restrained himself. It took masterful self-control and he plastered a confident smile on his face. "Me. You. You were naked, Barnes."

She took a sideways step, deftly moving out of his arm span. "You are such a pig."

There it was. The truth. His report had calculated an eighteen-percent reduction in operating expenses. All in labor. Including 44713. The *pig* tag was nothing less than he deserved, but he wished he didn't hurt. Nonetheless, his consultant's training served him well and his smile never wavered. "You want me."

"Oh, puh-lease."

"Have it your way," he said, just as the wooden door swung open.

A butterball in a tie brushed by them—Abercrombie, Adam presumed—and Adam gestured toward the open doorway of the now-empty room. "After you."

She seated herself at the far end of the conference table, a gray, modern monstrosity that looked as though it could seat forty. If he'd been smart, as he told himself he was, he would've sat down on the opposite end. Far away. But instead, he sat down right across from her. The better to hammer the final nail in his coffin.

One last come-on. One insinuating wink and they'd be history. He could write his report, go home, and he'd never have a chance to touch Jessica Barnes again.

Unfortunately, he'd have to meet her eyes if he wanted to crater the deal. On the far side of the floor, a power-drill revved up and down, as, screw by screw, a wall was sealed shut.

And to prove exactly what a spineless heel he was, he just couldn't do it.

A man with integrity would have taken his losses and lessons learned and walked away.

Adam shifted under the weight of his guilt. "You probably think I'm a weasel."

Damn it all, she didn't even hesitate to reply. "Yes."

This time he met her eyes. "Well, you'd be right."

"And don't forget smarmy," she said with a superior tone to her voice.

"That, too," he agreed.

"And a shark."

She was starting to get into this, and he didn't want to discourage her. "Yes."

"A Machiavellian German pinscher."

He supposed there were worse things than being compared to an overgrown terrier, and he sighed. "Are you done yet?"

"No."

Did he really expect her to say yes? Sapped of conversational energy he merely waved a "go on" hand.

"You're stuffy. And too neat."

Oddly enough, now he was more curious than insulted. "More issues we need to bring to the table?"

"I'm just getting warmed up," she said. Then a dark glower came over her face and she added, "You eat salads for lunch."

Startled, he looked at her, trying to decode that one. "Why is that an issue?"

"You wouldn't understand."

"And you aren't going to explain it?" The brown in her eyes sharpened and he shook his head. "Never mind. Is there more?"

She shifted her chair, one inch closer to him. "No. I think I'm done."

"Do you feel better?"

Jessica stared up at the ceiling, lips pouting in an eye-catching manner. "Yes. I think I do."

He stuck out his hand to her. "Adam Taylor. Glad to meet you."

She switched the folders to her left hand, and for the briefest of moments, her long fingers clung to his own. "Jessica Barnes. And don't think this is going to help you win the bet."

Right now he considered himself the greatest of fools for even accepting her bet in the first place. If ever there was a woman destined to hate him in the end, it was 44713, but he wondered if the time in between would be worth it.

When she smiled, he discovered the tiniest of dimples in her left cheek. Feeling absurdly pleased, he smiled back. "No. Us farm boys know when we're beat."

5

JESSICA PRETENDED to study her notes, trying not to glance at her watch. Adam was staring at her, making her intensely self-conscious, when all the while she wanted nothing more than to just lay down her spreadsheet and drown in his gorgeous gray-green eyes.

Every now and then he went and checked something on the computer set up at the head of the table. Every now and then her eyes followed him, secretly admiring the efficient movements when he walked.

A blue-uniformed maintenance worker came through the door and double-checked his clipboard. "This Conference Room G? Isn't it supposed to be empty?"

Jessica noticed the roll of cable he carried over his shoulder. At last, an Adam diversion. No bet-losing with cable guy watching over her shoulder. She smiled at the poor man in gratitude. "Yes."

Cable guy winked at her and made a clicking "hey girlie" noise with his tongue. This time she ignored both him and Adam, instead staring down at the tiny numbers on the spreadsheet.

Hard-Wire was in perfect financial health, just

needing a few cuts here and there. Revenues were growing at the projected rates and, all in all, it looked ripe for getting bought.

The whole thing sucked mightily and unfortunately Mr. Gorgeous Gray-Green Eyes seemed to be the man calling the shots.

Every time she thought she had him figured out, he threw her a curve. He had started out this morning the silver-tongued fox trying to charm his way into the egg basket, and had ended up the soft-spoken farm boy who she swore had actually blushed when she'd castigated his disgustingly healthy lunches.

How was a woman supposed to resist a man who blushed? She sneaked a peek at him from under her lashes. He seemed to be deeply engrossed in the papers in front of him.

The cable guy set up a ladder in the corner and began removing the ceiling panels. He threaded the wire through the fret-work in the ceiling, the whoosh-whoosh sound pleasantly annoying.

At least the bet was only for ten days. For ten days, she could resist Derek Jeter in a Cubs uniform—her own private fantasy.

The object of her resistance cleared his throat and she looked up. "Yes?"

He shook his head, looking a little sheepish. "Sorry. Need to get some water. Want something to drink?"

"Tea would be nice. Black, please."

Cable guy stopped the whoosh-whooshing. "Hey,

buddy? You mind bringing me a pop? Something diet."

Instead of looking annoyed, Adam smiled, very unsharklike. "Sure thing," he said easily, and walked out of the room with Jessica staring after him. There was something about a man in a white shirt and tailored pants that just made her squirm.

The cable guy started threading the cable again, humming "Stairway to Heaven" under his breath, completely spoiling the moment. Mad at herself for getting loopy again, Jessica checked her watch. Ten more minutes, surely she could last ten more minutes.

All too soon, Adam returned and set the Hard-Wire coffee mug down in front of her. He handed the pop to the cable guy and sat back quietly in his seat.

Jessica looked up, met his eyes and then quickly looked away.

All she needed to remember was that he was the Ax-man, and then think about all the hard work she'd done to land the perfect job.

Three years ago she had read an article in the paper on Hard-Wire and knew exactly what the founder, Artie Boodlesman was capable of. Her query letter to the company was informative and complimentary. She'd researched the financials of the company, learned more about network routers than she really wanted to know, and when she got the job, it had felt more like fait accompli than success.

This job was her destiny and Adam Taylor wanted to take it away. Against the soft conference-room chair, she felt her backbone grow two sizes larger. Stronger she may be, but she didn't make the mistake of looking at him again.

At exactly ten-thirty, Artie Boodlesman bounded through the doorway, raising the average IQ in the room to 200. "Who's he?" he asked, pointing to the maintenance worker on the ladder.

"Don't mind me. I'll be done here pronto. In fact, just need to check the outlet in the floor." The cable guy climbed down and crawled under the table.

"Where's Garrison?" Artie asked of no one in particular and immediately stood in front of the computer, his fingers flying over the keys like a concert pianist.

Walking in next was Garrison Reynolds, the CFO. "I'm here, Artie," Garrison answered. Always a good dresser, today he had outdone himself, nattily attired in his dark-gray Brooks Brothers suit and maroon tie. Garrison was Fortune 500 and maturity. The rudder for the Hard-Wire ship, and Hard-Wire was lucky to have him.

After Garrison seated himself, Artie looked up and nodded, but didn't smile. Artie never smiled and Jessica secretly thought it was because it made him look twelve years old. "All right. Let's start. Garrison? Next year's budget? Complete? What've we got?"

Garrison steepled his fingers in front of him, and thought over his answer carefully. He was a man who never said a word until he'd mulled it over—twice. "I'll have it to you by end of business today, Artie. Just want to double-check the numbers and reconcile our sales projections against the manufacturing costs."

"Fabulous. Jessica? Second-quarter revenue projections? Still on target?"

Jessica could recite the numbers in her sleep. "Over by 2.713 percent, sir."

"Excellent. Three-point-four would have been better."

"Yes, but with the downturn in the Asia-Pacific sector, we're anticipating a slowdown, although not a significant one. Less than one percent."

It was more than acceptable and Artie knew it. He bobbed his head. "All right. And one small change of plans. Jess, I'll need your help. Chicago Boys' and Girls' Club were looking for help in coaching a girls' track team. I volunteered you."

Jessica kept the shock from showing on her face. "Me?"

"Yes. You're the closest thing to a track coach we've got. Need the community-involvement angle here. Good PR. Lots of free press. You'll do great. It's a win-win."

She didn't want to hammer the point home, but she had never envisioned herself as a track coach. "You really want me to do it?"

Artie looked annoyed. *Bad move, J.* "Didn't I say so?"

There was no point in arguing any more. "Yes, sir. Count me in."

"Good. Delia will e-mail you the details with the

practice times and location and uniforms. You've got a coaches' class scheduled for tomorrow morning. Sorry to cut into your week. Coaches' training. Need to get you certified ASAP. Practice starts on Monday. We're counting on you."

"Yes, sir," she replied, with perhaps a hint of sarcasm, but no one seemed to detect it.

And then Artie turned to his own personal pièce de résistance. Adam. "Adam? The report?"

Adam smiled, confident, calm, the consummate professional—total shark. "All complete. I turned it over to my Q&A team this morning and you'll be receiving the summary by the end of next week."

Artie's eyes glittered. Everyone knew that he considered JCN the perfect answer to getting market acceptance. "Looking good?"

"Looks good, sir. The value proposition is solid."

This time Artie smiled. A genuine smile. He looked twelve, but a happy twelve. "Wowza. Anything you need from Hard-Wire, Adam?"

"No, sir. Everyone has been cooperative. The work's been seamless."

"If you have any questions on the financials, make sure you talk to Jessica. She'll have the answers you need."

Adam nodded to Artie, not looking at Jessica. "She's already been very accommodating, Artie."

Artie shot Jessica an approving glance. "Excellent. Jessica, good work. Anything Adam needs, you can take care of it, right?"

Jessica looked down at her paper, hoping no one would misread the hot flush on her cheeks. Artie wasn't talking about carnal needs, but the idea was still there, buried deep in the tombs of the graveyard for Lost Managers who were Never Going to Own a Porsche. Jessica sighed. "Yes, sir."

Artie slapped a hand on the table. "All right. We're done."

With great dignity, she picked up her things and headed for the door.

"Jessica."

Coolly she turned her head, giving him a sharp edge of shoulder. "Yes?"

"I'm sorry."

She smiled tightly and waited as a maintenance worker brushed by with a canvas tarp under his arm. When they were alone again, she spoke. "Tell it to the Pope."

He took her arm. "I wish I wasn't doing this."

Pretty words. He was a master of pretty words. She stared pointedly at his hand on her arm. "Then quit."

An office temp carrying a load of files under her arm brushed past them and Adam looked at Jessica in frustration. He opened the door to the stairwell and pulled her inside. "Damn it. Is there no place with privacy here?"

"We don't need to be having this conversation."

"I'm a consultant. I tell businesses how I think they can run better. I'm good at it. I know this is a bad idea." He brushed a hand through his hair, the dark strands ruffling in an appealing mess. "Why don't we call the bet off?"

He shouldn't be so smart, so cold-bloodedly logical. She couldn't think around him, alternating between bouts of lust and panic, and sometimes, when she thought of not seeing him again, the panic grew even worse—and he didn't looked panicked at all.

So she got angry. "Of all the egotistical clods. You think you're going to lose, and you can't bear the idea, can you? Why the hell would I ever want to go to bed with the man who is going to take away my career? Winning this bet is going to be a snap." To illustrate her point, Jessica snapped her fingers just as if she was snapping off her own foolish nature.

"You can just do that? You'd be a fool to deny what's going on between us."

"There's nothing going on." They both knew she was lying, which made her even madder.

"Then prove it."

"Anytime," she said, throwing down the gauntlet.

"Go out with me tonight," he said, picking up the gauntlet and shoving it neatly down her throat.

After a moment, Jessica realized her out. The truth. "I have plans."

And of course he didn't believe her. "Now isn't that convenient?"

"You think it's an excuse?" she snapped, mainly because it really was.

"You bet."

"Why?"

"Because you're afraid."

"Oh, you are such a, such a...*consultant*. You want a date? Sure!"

"I'll pick you up at seven. Casual."

Jessica opened the door to the stairwell, ignoring the receptionist's startled glance. "I'll be ready."

Adam followed out behind her. "Good."

WHEN SHE GOT BACK to her desk, the first thing she did was to check if Mickey was online. Thankfully, she found that her IM session showed Mickey active.

Jessica says: "You there?"

Mickey says: "Yupper."

Jessica says (whining): "I'm such a nimrod."

Mickey says (because she's a good friend and will listen to whining): "What now?"

Jessica says: "Date. Adam. Tonight."

Mickey says: "WHAT? You're supposed to help me find a birthday present for your mom."

Jessica says (crawling under desk): "I know. Sorry."

Mickey says: "Words, words, words. What's up with Adam? At this rate, you'll end up losing more than the bet."

Jessica says (thinking Mickey is experiencing a mild case of PMS): "Hardy-har-har. He thinks I can't resist him, so I'm going out with him to prove that I can."

Mickey says (with more than a mild case of PMS, bordering on the you-can't-handle-the-truth bitchiness that only real best friends are capable of): "J, even

Beth would see through that line of convoluted reasoning."

Jessica says (defensively): "It's true."

Mickey says: "Okay, shutting up now. I'll call Beth and see if she can help me, since you'll be busy resisting Adam. I'm calling your house at 11:00 p.m. If you're not there, it doesn't take a rocket scientist to find the right conclusion."

Jessica says (feeling abandoned and panicking): "Mick, what am I going to do?"

Mickey says: "You like your job?"

Jessica says (muttering more than truly speaking clearly): "You know the answer."

Mickey says: "Then help me pick out a gift and dump your date."

Jessica says (ignoring that): "Want to help me coach a track team?"

Mickey says: "You ask me that after you're standing me up tonight, with less than three hours' notice?"

Jessica says (tossing her head in denial): "Yes."

Mickey says: "No. You should dump your date, J. Not only would it solve this daily crisis, you'd get help with your track team, and I'd get a present. I don't see any problems with that."

Jessica says (while sneezing): "I like him."

Mickey says: "Well, there's two problems with that. First, he's going to ax your job. Second, he's going to ax your job."

Jessica says (crap, crap, crap): "That's only one."

Mickey says (in that annoying know-it-all tone of

one who is usually right): "But it's a big one, don't you think?"

Jessica says (I'm toast): "Gotta go, M. TTFN."

Mickey says: "Toodles."

Jessica twirled her chair around and stared through the wall of glass. Adam was there, just across the way, cell phone in hand, pacing about his office. He'd rolled his shirtsleeves up to his elbows and she noticed what nice forearms he had. Even now he was probably plotting the demise of the entire finance department, consolidating operations, defining efficiencies, and all that other craporama that men like him spewed so well.

Men with nice forearms.

She rolled her eyes and chided herself for judging a man solely on his physical attributes. A man needed depth, character...

He turned around and she noticed the way his pants just clung so perfectly to his...

Ah, crap, crap, crap.

ADAM SHOWED UP at her door at exactly 7:00 p.m. Not early, not late. Punctual.

Normally she abhorred punctual men because she was usually six minutes late. Tonight she'd been ready for forty-five minutes.

It'd taken her less than fifteen minutes to settle on jeans and her favorite white sweater, and judging from his own jeans and button-down, she'd chosen right.

"Where're we heading?" she asked, as they rode down the elevator to the garage.

"It's a surprise," was all that he would tell her, opening the door and waiting as she settled inside the car. The Porsche. His Porsche.

Tonight she let him drive. It seemed only fitting since, after all, it *was* his car. The engine purred more beautifully than normal and Jessica wondered if she'd ever hear the purr of a 320-horsepower Porsche engine again. Every day it seemed less and less likely.

Traffic was busy for a Friday evening, and they followed the lines of the city. Apartment buildings towered into the sky, casting long shadows along the streets. The El roared overhead as it barreled along the tracks, and at each corner was a saloon.

A neighborhood tavern where the vastness of the world disappeared, to be replaced by a universe bounded by one square mile. Where Bears fans discussed the merits of Gale Sayers and Walter Payton. Where the greatness of Chicago could be tasted in the cold bite of the beer.

Jessica looked at the profile of Adam and wondered how a man who lived by his words survived in a town that thrived on its deeds.

He turned to her, questioning her look, and she shrugged. There would be time for that later, for now they had arrived.

At Bowlland. Yes, that's right folks, Bowlland.

There it was, spelled out in ten-foot-high neon-pink letters—including two *l*s.

Gee willikers, he'd taken her to a bowling alley.

"Do you bowl?" she asked pseudo-casually.

"Of course. You?"

"Some," she answered, knowing she'd never lifted a ball in her life, although she did remember watching some of the Pro Bowlers Tour when she was a kid. Even now she was searching the dim recesses of her memory because she was *so* not going to make a fool of herself tonight.

Still, *bowling?* Okay, maybe resisting Adam Taylor was going to be easier than she imagined.

He came around and opened her door, and then they went inside.

The first thought to pop into her head was "Wow." The room was black, the lanes were long lines of purple punctuated at the end with ten white pins that gleamed like capped teeth. Lights flashed in a whirl of color, and somewhere, she was sure, there was a disco ball.

Definitely not Pro Bowlers Tour.

And there was music. Loud music. Even the traditional bowling sounds were drowned out by—rap. Yes, it was definitely rap. Something about love and cops and raining money.

She turned to Adam and noticed her white sweater was now glowing purple. Not the look she had wanted. He had chosen to wear blue, which looked nice.

"This is different," she said, holding her hand up to the black lights.

"I've never been here before, but I thought it sounded safe."

"Safe?"

He smiled that unassuming farm-boy smile and she felt a tiny tremor in her stomach, the first sure sign of backbone shrinkage. "I just thought we wouldn't get into any trouble here, you know?"

That she understood. He was being sensible. Okay, it wasn't exactly the evening she had wanted—secretly wanted, that is. But he was right. How much trouble could you get into while bowling under black lights? She nodded, sagelike. "Very smart, Taylor."

His smile turned into a full-fledged grin. "Ready to kick my ass, Barnes?"

"Always." When they were competing, she could handle it, and she made herself forget all about Hard-Wire, Porsches and pink slips.

The bowling shoes had white laces that glowed fluorescent purple, and they rented balls that glowed as well. He laughed when she picked out a yellow ten-pounder, but she stuck to her guns. Yellow was her lucky color. They bought some drinks and then headed for lane fourteen. The alley was filled with crowds of kids and teenagers and a few hard-core leaguers whose personalized bowling shirts blazed in the flashing lights.

Above each lane was a computerized scoring screen, complete with a little computerized man who would shout or groan appropriately. At the head of the lane were the requisite plastic chairs and mounted table.

At last it was show time. Jessica picked up the ball just as she'd seen Mark Roth do it on TV, and guided it lovingly to the line. The ball left her hand, gliding smoothly down the lane, a straight yellow arrow, heading down, down...

It started to veer to the left and she fanned her hand in the air, willing the ball to the right, to the right, to the right...

And gutter.

She stood, hands on hips, trying to understand what had gone wrong.

The little computer man groaned. That could get very old, very fast.

From behind her, she heard Adam's voice. Deep, sexy and not a bit of superiority in his tone. "Would you like a few tips?"

Her nose began to tickle and she searched her pockets for a tissue. Before she truly erupted, he shoved one into her hand and when she had regained control of her breathing she headed back to her seat. "Thank you for the tissue. As for the tips, they aren't necessary," she replied primly and then sat down on the plastic seat.

He, of course, bowled like a professional. The classic slide, the perfect release, the ball gliding down like an arrow.

A straight arrow.

And of course, he got a strike. Annoyingly enough,

the little man on the computerized scoreboard jumped up and down. *"Strike!"*

Jessica smiled politely.

This time, she was determined to improve. She carefully took aim, willed her arm to stay straight, pulled back, began the approach and boom...the ball began its journey.

Straight. Straight. Straight. Left.

But at least she was saved the embarrassment of a gutter ball. She knocked down two pins. The little computerized man grinned.

She thought about climbing up and hammering that little computerized man with one of the pins left standing, but satisfied herself with an evil glare. With her second ball, she clipped one pin, making it wobble but, as if glued to the floor, it stayed upright.

On Adam's next turn, he knocked down seven pins. A measly seven pins. She smiled. "Better luck next time."

And then he pulled a spare.

Jessica knocked down three pins and then the next ball ended up in the gutter. Gradually she was learning to tune out the little computer man.

After she made her way back to her seat, Adam leaned forward, sexier than a man in bowling shoes ever had a right to be. "Are you sure I can't help you?"

It was the sincere look in his eyes that got to her. Not the smooth polished veneer that she usually saw at work. She squirmed in her seat, uncomfortable with the idea of trusting him. "You really want to? You didn't just dream up this little exercise for retribution?"

"Actually, I did this for my own sanity. I needed to leave you alone and this seemed like the best way. I like my competitions to be fair, not one-sided. It takes all the fun out of winning."

Jessica took a sip of her drink and considered him over the edge of the glass. It should have been more humiliating than it was, but he seemed genuine. "I'd like some lessons."

He looked pleased and she realized she'd done the right thing.

This time when she made the long walk to the line, Adam accompanied her.

"Okay, here's what you do." He put his arm around her and she felt a sneeze coming on. She stepped back, willed the sneeze away and then returned to his warmth.

Her mind drifted off the game and into a whirlpool of pure sensual lust.

Gently he pulled her arm back, and showed her how to straighten her wrist. He was all business, and she was all goo. Very demeaning. She shook off the aftereffects, concentrating on the pins in front of her. When she was ready, she took a few steps forward, let the ball go, and then—

Boom. Six pins down. The little computer man cheered.

Adam put an arm around her. A friendly, comradely arm that made her want to stay there. "Excellent!"

His praise felt good. For a moment she stood, let herself bask in his shadow, and then she shook off the momentary weakness. "You've done it now, Taylor."

"You think you can beat me?"

"Do farm boys fly?"

He started to laugh. "Barnes, you're trouble, did anybody ever tell you that?"

"Just my mom."

"You got four pins left. Do me proud."

She winked at him and took off for the line. This time her execution was flawless. She only got another two pins, but above her head, the computerized man jumped up and down and looked as happy as she was feeling.

By the time they had played ten frames, Adam was ahead by thirty-seven pins. Not exactly her finest moment, but she didn't care.

He stayed behind her for six frames. By the end of frame four, she had started to get the hang of it, but she didn't say anything because she liked the feel of his body behind her, and he didn't seem to notice that her delivery was improving.

Which was fine by her.

6

IN THE seventh frame, she bowled a strike, but Adam was too busy watching her to notice at first. He moved from behind her, but he couldn't go far. So he watched the way her face froze with concentration as the ball rolled down the lane. Then as the pins rocked and fell, her eyes lit up and she glowed. A more cynical man would have said that it was the lighting, but Adam had seen Jessica under all sorts of lighting now, and she really, truly glowed.

What sort of dynamics did it take to make someone glow?

She turned to him, her smile too inviting to refuse, and it would have taken more than forty of Old Man Cabbott's stubbornest horses to keep him from kissing her.

Jessica didn't resist, merely closed her eyes and kissed him back, her energy charging into his body. The music cranked up to something loud and infernal, the sound of balls hitting pins crashed all around them, but inside his head, he could only hear the soft flow of her breathing. He was listening for it, like a sailor following a siren's song. Her compact body fit his so perfectly, and he didn't stop his arms from curving around her, pulling her even closer.

They stayed that way for some time. Lips meeting lips in a gentle sharing of souls. For Adam, it was a moment of blinding truth. He had known from the first day he saw her that he wanted Jessica Barnes in his bed. But now, when her mouth was clinging to his so desperately, he knew he wanted her in his life.

He wanted her energy, her purpose. He wanted to be the reason she glowed. His mother would have said it was mighty selfish to be having such ideas about a woman when he was going to destroy her very dreams, but Adam had never had his mother's strength, only his father's convictions.

When she pulled away from him—hesitatingly, he liked to think—he pushed the soft strands of her hair away from her face, making sure the glow was still there, that he hadn't stolen it from her. It was.

She laughed, a little nervously, and made light of the moment. "I thought bowling was safe," she said, reminding him of his intentions, and Adam stepped back away from her, trying to think of some way to remake his future. Lacking any brilliant ideas, he asked her if she'd like something to eat instead.

The diner was like a million other bowling-alley restaurants. Coffee that sat on the hot-plate for hours, beer that was so cold there were chips of ice in it, and a hot dog that you would sell your soul for.

Cora, the waitress, was an older woman who'd probably been here when the doors first opened. She seated them at a table and proudly placed the plastic-covered menus on the plastic red-checked tablecloth.

After they ordered, Adam debated politics and religion with Jessica. It seemed a better choice than the weather and he wasn't fool enough to bring up work. It came as no surprise that she was a Democrat and he was a Republican. He preached to her about the evils of union labor, and she proudly informed him that her father was a card-carrying member of the Ironworkers Local Union #47. He had been raised Southern Baptist, one of the God-fearing people, and she was a fourth-generation Catholic who went to mass every Sunday.

It was a match made in hell, and he couldn't remember when he'd had a better time.

It took less than ten minutes for Cora to come back with two well-dressed hot dogs, fries and a couple of beers, and Jessica eyed the food with an appreciative glance, then took a bite out of the loaded dog.

For a minute, Adam watched her eat. She ate the way she did everything. With enthusiasm and gusto.

She noticed him watching and a blush ran up her cheeks. After she had swallowed, she shrugged unapologetically. "Sue me. I like to eat."

That made him laugh. "I don't mind at all," he said, taking a bite himself. It was gooey and sticky, and if he'd been with a client, he'd have used a fork to cut it up into small bites. Tonight he was a hands-on kinda guy.

"So, have you always liked to bowl?" she said, sipping her beer, a bit of foam settling on her lower lip. It was a tempting sight, and he took a minute before he remembered to answer.

"My uncle Dave owned a bowling alley when I was a kid, so Ma and me bowled for free. Seems like there was never enough time to go, but we managed to get out there some. Ma was the real pro in the family, but she taught me some of her tricks."

"Your mom still in Alabama?"

"Nah. She died a couple of years ago."

"I'm sorry." Jessica looked genuinely sad, and he wished his mom could have met her. They would have argued for days on end, but she would have loved Jessica.

"Thanks. Both your parents still around?"

She laughed and picked up a French fry. "Oh, yeah. Mom's got her fiftieth birthday coming up in a few months. You know anything about string quartets?"

He looked up in midbite, curious. "Not a thing."

"Too bad," she said, but before he could probe further, she switched the subject. "How's the book club coming?"

"I haven't been."

"I bet the ladies are heartbroken."

That was a statement he wasn't going to go near. He'd gotten a couple of phone calls, although if his shoes weren't so polished or his car so flashy, he wondered if they would have bothered. He had sown the seeds of his image so meticulously, yet hadn't bothered to check the quality of the crops he was growing.

"Why do you do it?" she asked, and he started.

Then he realized she was still talking about the book club.

He thought for a minute, considering the consultant's answer. Maybe it was the beer talking, but in the end he settled for gut-level honesty. "It's tough meeting people when you're always traveling around and your assignments never last more than the time it takes to go to contract. I get to know a lot of hotel clerks and restaurant folks."

"You don't say that with a smile on your face," she said, watching him with a sharp gaze that was unsettling.

"I don't know. I get to see different parts of the country, get to find the out-of-the-way places, get to see a lot of interesting businesses. It's actually pretty nice."

She settled back in her seat and eyed him suspiciously. "Well, I would hate it."

"That's why you're in finance," he said, as if personality made his job palatable.

"Don't *you* hate it sometimes?"

Adam pretended to be shocked. "Of course not."

And of course, she didn't buy it for a minute. "Oh, come on. You can't tell me that once you meet a few of the faces that you're about to whack off the payroll, you get all warm and fuzzy. Or are you one of those guys that's into pain?"

He chose to ignore the pain comment. Truth was, his conscience was only now waking up from a long, dead sleep. "That part's not too fun."

They ate in silence, and he polished off the last of his dog and fries.

"So, you finished the report?"

He nodded. He had scheduled a meeting for tomorrow morning. A preliminary presentation to JCN. His hot dog was sitting heavy in his gut.

"We're a good candidate for the buyout, aren't we?"

Again with the head nod.

Jessica's nose twitched and he waited for the sneeze, but it never came. Instead, she studied her hot dog.

"Do you think these are healthy?"

He thought about lying to her, just to make her feel good, make her think everything would be all right, but he couldn't. "No," he answered.

Her smile never wavered, her glow never receded. It was as if nothing could shake Jessica Barnes from her dogged pursuit of life.

Rather she stood, crumpled her napkin on the table. "Ready for me to whoop your butt?"

"You betcha." He wadded up his napkin, took a last swig of beer, and just for the hell of it, wiped the back of his hand across his mouth.

The good Lord willing, life was contagious.

THEY BOWLED two more games, but then the lights went back up, the dedicated bowlers arrived, and the fun went out of the night. Jessica thought her score had improved significantly, from forty-seven to eighty-five, all in a mere three hours. She shivered with pure pleasure at the thought of what she could do with serious practice.

Adam Taylor would be toast. Of course, it'd take quite a bit of practice to beat his lowest score of one-fifty, but she was willing to try. Of course, he'd also be gone by the time she broke one hundred.

No way around it, it was depressing.

The ride home was silent. It wasn't the good, sexual-awareness sort of silence that normally accompanied a date. This was more of an I-really-need-to-stay-away-from-you sort of silence.

Going out with the Ax-man gave her an odd feeling. Every now and then she had to call him that in her head, just to remind herself that he wasn't the man of her dreams. He wasn't so funny or so charming or so terribly sexy that it would change the intrinsic badness in the situation.

All her hopes regarding vice president—climbing up the corporate ladder at a company she'd helped make—were being knocked down by a man who bowled one-fifty.

Love Bites wasn't just a T-shirt slogan.

By the time he pulled into the garage, Jessica had regained her normal sensibilities and she opened the car door before he could turn off the fine-tuned engine. "Don't worry about walking me up. I'll be fine."

He held out a hand to her in protest. Open-palmed, a gesture all the more deadly for its restraint.

She shook her head. "Trust me on this. I need to go up alone."

Stubbornly he persisted. "I wasn't brought up to let a woman walk herself to her door. I'll behave myself, if that's what you're worried about."

"It's not you, it's me." And before she could think, she placed one hand into his, and tried to ignore how good it felt. She met his gaze, his eyes shadowed, but it wasn't so dark that she could miss the intensity there. In the deepest recesses of her heart, she wanted to believe he would change, wanted to believe that her life would not, but this time she thought her deep recesses were wrong. And it hurt.

In the distance, a car horn echoed in the garage and the intensity faded. He placed a warm kiss in her palm and closed her fingers around it. "Take care, Jess."

"See you in the morning."

"See you then."

He watched from the car as she made her way to the elevator. Behind the lights of the garage, his face was a shadow. When the doors opened she stepped in and scanned the shadows one last time. Still, he was watching her. She couldn't see him, but she felt his gaze. Slowly the doors closed and she pushed the button to her floor.

With her backbone firmly returned to the locked and upright position, she leaned back against the wall of the elevator and rode up to the twenty-second floor.

All alone.

THE NEXT MORNING, Jessica walked through the revolving door at the Oakmont Towers building at exactly eight o'clock. As she did every morning, she ducked behind the monstrous metal sculpture in the lobby to switch from her walking shoes to heels and straighten her silk blouse and skirt. Then she followed in the line of suits to the elevator banks. The second bank went to Tower II, Floors 11-25. Patiently she waited, the crowd behind her gathering, the morning conversations a low buzz of greetings and business.

The display above the elevator had just flashed to 7 when she felt him behind her. He wasn't touching her, but she could smell his cologne and her heartbeat pumped in double-time. She waited for him to speak, didn't want to act as if she knew he was behind her, as if he was affecting her so strongly. So she continued to stare up at the little circle where the numbers began to flash in descending order—slowly. So very slowly.

At last the elevator doors opened, and immediately the knot of suits flowed into the confines. She took the far corner near the front, not to escape, but to see if he would follow. When he did, she didn't allow herself to smile.

"Good morning, Jessica," he said, always the consummate professional.

"Hello, Adam. I didn't see you get on," she lied, then looked forward to watch the doors shut, shutting him out as well. The melodic voice in the elevator called out the number of each floor as they slid smoothly upward. And it was on the third floor that his wool suit-jacket skimmed against her arm.

On the sixth floor, when the three suits in the back shouldered their way forward to exit, he pressed up against her, the powerful lines of his back just brushing the tips of her breasts. Her nipples peaked instantly under the thin silk of her blouse, and Jessica felt a swell of pressure pulse between her legs. The rough material brushed against her, once, twice, the small contact enough to make her shudder, still longing for more.

Then the doors closed, and he stood away from her, the distance between them reestablished.

For the remaining eight floors she held her breath, her body eager for just one more touch, one accidental press of skin. She didn't dare look in his direction, but out of the corner of her eye, she could trace the tiny hollow below his ear and she memorized the way that his dark hair lightened to a golden brown just at the very tips.

When she closed her eyes, she could smell the subtle musk of his cologne, a faint trace of soap, and beneath it all, the scent that belonged uniquely to him.

The elevator voice gently cooed, "Fourteen," and Jessica awoke from her fog. Adam waited for her to exit first, and she brushed past him. Not because of the tight confines, merely because she needed to touch him one last time.

THE CHICAGO OFFICE of Kearney, Markham and Williams was in a high-rise in the financial district. In this day and age, consultants didn't have offices of their own, but instead reserved offices and meeting rooms at the companies they were advising. Adam had arrived a couple of hours early to double-check that the video-conference equipment was in place, to make sure the copy of the presentation had arrived at the San Jose headquarters of JCN and to have a pre-presentation planning session with two of the partners from his firm.

The senior partner, Philip Osterson, was handling the JCN account and was anxious to see the recommendations that Adam had made. Osterson was a stickler for details and was famous for his customer skills. Fortune had done a profile on him once, calling him the Next Generation Consultant. So, at nine-thirty, Adam found himself seated in the conference room, bagel and coffee in hand, discussing what was rapidly becoming his least favorite subject.

"You've indicated that fifteen percent can be cut from the operational side of the house. Twelve percent in labor, and the remaining three percent in redundant expenses. That's good, but we need to do better. And JCN wants their engineering team intact, so we need to respect that in our proposals. Come on, Adam. I've seen you cut twenty-five percent with your eyes closed."

Adam stared into the black recesses of his coffee cup, desperately holding on to the "let's ignore the bottom line" position. "If they utilize JCN's operation base and merge their ERP systems, they could recognize two-percent cuts in year one, and then ten percent thereafter. JCN will want to do the systems consolidation as soon as possible. Hard-Wire's still young enough that they haven't gone overboard on customizing. Hell, some of the accounting is still done on spreadsheets, but that's to JCN's advantage."

Osterson listened, but his eyes glimmered behind the wire-frame glasses. Opportunity was there, and Osterson knew it. "Marketing?"

"I would suggest they keep Garrison Reynolds. He could help ease the transition in culture and he's been an anchor for the upper management at Hard-Wire, helped them weather through the tech bust intact."

Osterson shook his head in admiration. Consultants didn't live in the trenches, and therefore had a high level of idol worship for those who did—and survived it. "Amazing story. Everyone else is floundering, and they're expanding their base, and adding fifty additional headcounts, forty in engineering, ten in production."

"Yes, sir. They have a good product and everyone knows it."

Osterson took another long look at the org chart. "Production will have to go. JCN will want to take that in-house."

Adam poured one package of sugar in his coffee, and watched the white crystals dissolve. "Yes, sir. That's in the report."

"Can we get them to a twenty-percent cut in operating expenses? That's JCN's Holy Grail. If we get them there, it's a done deal. What about finance?"

Adam took a long sip of coffee, letting the caffeine rip through his system. He could run on autopilot when necessary, and today it was necessary. "Standard. Payroll, accounting, budget. They're lean to begin with. I'm not sure that'll get you any major cost savings." Still he defended her. He was losing the war, and she'd never know that he put up a fight.

"Well, it's a start, and that's low-hanging fruit, so might as well take them out."

Adam met Osterson's gaze evenly, needing to keep the option in play. "Philip, I'm not sure about that. I think we should consider keeping them on until the systems consolidation is complete. You know how these things are. The legacy stuff is always a bitch to understand, and in the end, it might save JCN some serious headaches."

And Osterson didn't bite. Of course, Philip knew how the game was played. Adam had learned almost everything from him. "I know. All good points, Adam. Let's get a read from JCN on what their concerns are with regard to consolidation. If they're not worried about it, why should we be? In the meantime, we really need to shoot for twenty percent."

Adam watched as Osterson drew a red line through finance. He took another long, numbing sip of coffee. Somehow he'd make it up to her.

"Legal?" asked Philip.

"All done through outsourcing. They've hired their

own counsel while they're in negotiation with JCN, but after the takeover is complete, that will go away."

"Marketing?"

The process became easier, the faces turning into numbers. Adam took out his pen and marked off slots. "There's some potential there. Marketing accounts for five percent of the nonengineer payroll. Other than Reynolds, the whole department can be disincluded."

"Sales?"

"Smaller than marketing because Hard-Wire has spent most of its preproduction man-hours focused on identifying its customer base and building the product accordingly. There's five on the sales team, with a 2003 budget of $400,000."

Adam continued. For thirty minutes, Philip sat with a pen in hand, marking through budgets and head counts, and Adam felt the rock in his stomach getting bigger and bigger. So many times before, he'd sat through sessions exactly like this, pen in hand, working through extra head counts as if it was the Sunday-morning crossword puzzle.

"Problem, Taylor?"

Adam shook his head, shook off his conscience, and smiled grimly. "No, sir."

"Good. We've got another $2 million to find, and then we're good to go."

Adam studied the budgets in front of him, pulled out his notes, and slowly worked through the list of recommendations. It took thirty minutes to go through them all, but when they were done, they'd found the $2 million. Hard-Wire was lighter by $8 million per year for years one through five with a cut in headcount of exactly fifty-eight positions, including 44713.

The conference call with JCN went exactly as planned. Osterson was pleased, JCN was pleased and Adam would get a nice bonus when the whole deal was inked.

After they had hung up with JCN, Adam packed up his computer and his notes and headed for the door. Osterson stopped him on the way out. "Fine job, Adam. I think everything is going to work out."

Adam forced a smile. "Sure it is."

As LUCK would have it, he didn't escape cleanly. A rookie, Pete O'Connell, rode down with him on the elevator. O'Connell held the hungry gleam of a ladder-climber in his eyes, someone who handpicked his mentors carefully, using it as a career move as well as a learning experience.

O'Connell had picked Adam. So, what could you say? The boy had taste.

"Great weather," Pete commented, glancing out the glass elevator into the clear blue Chicago sky.

"Seems like it," answered Adam, glad to see Pete was learning so well.

O'Connell had gotten a Harvard MBA two years ago and he did the Ivy League school proud. He was ambitious, quick and a chameleon with his clients. After all, he had learned from one of the best.

"You have time for coffee?"

Adam checked his watch. He had a meeting scheduled with Artie at two—a status update. Although he knew Artie would be ecstatic, it was Jessica that Adam dreaded seeing.

How to explain to her that she wasn't going to make vice president? Oh, yeah, she'll get two or three months' severance pay and a sterling letter of recommendation, but the Porsche?

"Yeah, I've got time for coffee. How's the world of health care?"

When they made it to the lobby, they found two stools at the coffee bar and Adam sat patiently while Pete picked his brain on various issues: Was there an impending crisis in the health sector? What would it take for the financial sector to turn around? How to avoid career sluggishness?

Sadly enough, for every question, Adam had an answer.

Idly he sipped his coffee—third cup of the day— and watched the enthusiasm that Pete brought to the table. On most days Adam was just like that. What was it about the Hard-Wire job that stuck in his craw? Why did he feel like the loneliest man on the planet?

"You think the Bears will go all the way?"

Adam blinked, and realized he hadn't been listening. A fatal flaw in his line of work. What had Pete said? "That's a really good question," he answered automatically. "I'm glad you've asked it."

Pete stared at him in confusion and Adam continued.

"If you take both sides of the issue, and weigh the pros and cons, the risk equation, the added value of each position, then the answer becomes obvious."

Pete raised one brow. "How do you weigh the risk equation of the Bears' chances this year?"

Adam put on his I'm-wiser-than-you face. "Oh, I was just testing you. Seeing if you were paying attention. Obviously you were."

Thirty minutes later, Adam found himself an out and headed for the parking garage, coffee in hand, but he got caught for the second time.

Charles slipped into the garage elevator just as Adam pressed the P3 button.

Charles jabbed the P5 button with his briefcase. "Haven't seen you around much. Saw on your schedule you'd be coming into the office and I was hoping you'd drop by."

Against his white dress shirt, Charles looked tanned and happy, just like a man should look after returning from two weeks in the Virgin Islands.

"How was the honeymoon?" Adam asked, avoiding the "hoping you'd drop by" comment.

"Too short, my friend. Far too short. I could stay there forever."

"Would be nice."

"I saw the first call was scheduled with JCN this morning. Things proceeding there?"

"It's early yet."

"You've got that gleam in your eye, Adam."

Sadly enough, Adam suspected he did. Even now, when he was dreading seeing Jessica, he felt the hum of exhilaration, the thrill of the kill. "We'll see," he said, with a non-committal shrug.

"Hey, did you ever hook up with Jessica? If you'd like I can ask her over for dinner. Annie's not much of a cook, but we'll have to work on that. And there's always catering."

"I haven't had much time for a social life. The project is keeping me pretty busy and I want to stay focused."

"What? You got some little honey back home in Georgia? Is that why you're dragging your feet here?"

"Honest, Charles, there's no honey in Georgia. It's Alabama, not Georgia, and there's no honey in Alabama either. I'm just here to do a job, and then go home."

Charles just laughed. "I was just trying to help out a co-worker. Don't you think she's hot? She was out at a happy hour with Annie one time and was wearing this clingy dress thing. She dropped her wallet and bent over and I'm thinking to myself, Charles, that woman's ass was just made to—"

The coffee took off with a mind of its own. And there was Charles, with a nice, steaming hot coffee stain right down the front of his white shirt.

Adam put down his briefcase and pretended to be concerned. "Oh, geez. I can't believe I did that. It's been a long couple of weeks, and these muscle spasms are getting worse." He held up a shaking hand. "Would you look at that?"

By now Charles looked more than a little mad. "Well hey, you should be more careful. Go to a hospital, man. See a doctor. You can't go around with that kind of condition."

The elevator doors whooshed open and Adam took a step out. "You need a spare shirt? I've got one in the trunk of my car."

Charles paled under his tan. "No. I'll just go home. It's almost lunchtime. See a doctor. You need to get that taken care of. Somebody could get hurt."

Adam felt in his pocket for his keys and waved just as the doors whooshed shut. "I'll call and set up an appointment right now."

And at last he was safe.

THERE WAS a time when he would have been over the moon after a meeting like that. Cost-cutting measures drove his bonus structure. Streamlined efficiencies bought a Porsche. Hell, he was living the American Dream.

You feeling proud of yourself, boy? asked a familiar voice in his head.

"Leave me be," he whispered.

What are you doing, Adam?

"This is not something that you'd understand. Businesses don't run on bleeding hearts—"

And I was talking about spilling coffee all over that poor man.

"Do they really let you lie up there? Aren't there rules against that?"

You don't need to drag my reputation through the mud. You're the one that's stepping into the cow pastures, boy.

Adam cranked up the volume on the stereo and prayed that, just for today, the commute would be short. Of course, there was road construction going on.

"I have a talent for what I do."

Well, I hope you have more than one.

"It's not the best of times now, Ma. A man needs to be flexible and open to new opportunities."

She really likes you, Adam. In spite of everything you're going to do to her, she cares about you.

And then it occurred to him that the solution was right there in front of him. What if she wasn't supposed to be in Chicago? Maybe he was supposed to rescue her. He could bring her down to Alabama and marry her—

Marriage? You've been drinking too much coffee, son. You're going to be lucky if she talks to you once this deal is done, much less marries you.

God, he was just being silly.

No less silly than a boy talking to his dead mother every time he gets stuck in traffic. You're going to have to do the right thing, Adam.

The right thing? Who knew what that was? He had a house in Alabama that needed somebody to take care of it. He wanted to have someone waiting for him when he got home from a trip. Jessica was going to need somebody when this whole thing was done. It wasn't his fault that JCN was going to buy Hard-Wire. It wasn't his fault that JCN's accounting department was already two percent overstaffed. That's just the way things happened. Maybe this time instead of keeping his mind closed to what was happening around him, he could do some good.

A Ford Explorer with a Whirled Peas bumper sticker roared past, horn beeping incessantly, and Adam tried to concentrate on the road, which was difficult with his ma pestering him.

Sounds like you've got it all figured out, said the voice in his head.

"Yeah, I do." When he stated it aloud, it seemed the perfect solution. He'd wanted a wife, wanted someone who would be there for him, and he liked Jessica.

He couldn't be around her without thinking about making love to her. It was fate. Suddenly, the sun seemed to shine just a little bit brighter. He drummed his fingers on the steering wheel. "Yes, I do."

Looks like that lane is fixing to open up again, I'd best let you get back to your driving. And Adam—

Already he was thinking, planning. "Yeah, Ma?"

I think that Charles is going to remember that stunt. Somebody needed to teach him that you don't talk trash about a lady. You did good.

"Anytime."

OFFICIAL OPINION POLL

ANSWER 3 QUESTIONS AND WE'LL SEND YOU
2 FREE BOOKS AND A FREE GIFT!

DETACH AND MAIL CARD TODAY!

YOUR OPINION COUNTS!

Please check TRUE or FALSE below to express your opinion about the following statements:

Q1 Do you believe in "true love"?

"TRUE LOVE HAPPENS ONLY ONCE IN A LIFETIME."
- ○ TRUE
- ○ FALSE

Q2 Do you think marriage has any value in today's world?

"YOU CAN BE TOTALLY COMMITTED TO SOMEONE WITHOUT BEING MARRIED."
- ○ TRUE
- ○ FALSE

Q3 What kind of books do you enjoy?

"A GREAT NOVEL MUST HAVE A HAPPY ENDING."
- ○ TRUE
- ○ FALSE

YES, I have scratched the area below.

Please send me the 2 **FREE BOOKS** and **FREE GIFT** for which I qualify. I understand I am under no obligation to purchase any books, as explained on the back of this card.

342 HDL DZ4A   142 HDL DZ4Q

FIRST NAME   LAST NAME

ADDRESS

APT.#   CITY

STATE/PROV.   ZIP/POSTAL CODE

www.eHarlequin.com

(H-T-03/04)

The Harlequin Reader Service® — Here's how it works:

Accepting your 2 free books and gift places you under no obligation to buy anything. You may keep the books and gift and return the shipping statement marked "cancel." If you do not cancel, about a month later we'll send you 4 additional books and bill you just $3.57 each in the U.S., or $4.24 each in Canada, plus 25¢ shipping & handling per book and applicable taxes if any.* That's the complete price and — compared to cover prices of $4.25 each in the U.S. and $4.99 each in Canada — it's quite a bargain! You may cancel at any time, but if you choose to continue, every month we'll send you 4 more books, which you may either purchase at the discount price or return to us and cancel your subscription.

*Terms and prices subject to change without notice. Sales tax applicable in N.Y. Canadian residents will be charged applicable provincial taxes and GST.

7

WHEN ADAM walked through the doors at Hard-Wire, there was a spring in his step, because now he was the man with the plan. He didn't know why he hadn't seen it before. He'd spent so much time focusing on his requirements list that he'd overlooked Jessica's potential. She was intelligent, driven and sexy as hell. His heart knew that she'd be absolutely perfect.

First stop, her office.

He knocked on the door and was rewarded with a value-added smile that said she'd been thinking about him. If he leaned against the doorframe with more than a little confidence, well, who's to say that's cocky?

"Come out with me to lunch?" he asked.

She raised her chin, her eyes dancing. "The meeting must have gone well."

First punch, right below the belt. Adam smiled with more than a little effort. That was the trouble with Jessica—she would definitely be high-maintenance. "Can we not talk about it? Come to lunch," he wheedled, not a man to be overcome by a little resistance.

"Where?"

More acquiescence. That was good. "There's a quiet place I know in Arlington Heights. We can talk."

"That doesn't seem safe," she countered.

Adam sighed. God, he hated to admit it, but his mom was right. Marriage seemed like a long, long way away. That's okay, though, they had time.

He sank into her office chair, needing to close the distance between them. He searched for words and kept on tossing out what popped into his head. Finally he turned off the analysis and dived right in. "I'm tired of safe, Jessica. I wanted to talk to you in the elevator this morning and I couldn't. And it drove me nuts. Look, I don't know what's going to happen with Hard-Wire, but I do know what I want to happen with us."

Warily, she met his eyes, not that he could blame her. "And what's that?"

Adam leaned forward, searching for the beginnings of trust in her gaze, and finding something that just might have been it. "I want to be with you. I want to know more about you. I want to talk to you without walking around on eggshells because of the situation we're in."

"The situation we're in?" she repeated, just to make him uncomfortable.

He barreled forward, because he was making a little progress and knew it. Every large disconnect is solved one brick at a time. "I've never wanted a woman so much in my life. You're like some song that keeps buzzing around in my head. It won't let me go, Jessica."

"Exactly what are you asking here?"

More questions. She didn't believe he was actually pouring out his heart now. Instead, she was skeptical. Not that she really should trust him, but it burned him that she didn't.

He pushed back his chair and stood, then began to pace. Everything he wanted to tell her sounded so trite and overdone. She sat, coolly watching him, waiting.

At last, he began to speak. Haltingly at first.

"I want to spend as much time with you as possible. I want to go out with you. I want to make love to you so bad that I can't think straight anymore. I'm sitting in a conference room and I'm not thinking about damned budgets or streamlining business processes, I'm thinking about you lying beneath me. I woke up this morning dreaming you were there beside me. When I realized it'd just been a dream, it hurt. It physically hurt. Normally, I'm grounded and rational and logical, but I'm going out of my mind here."

For a long time she met his eyes, searching for the truth, and he hoped she could see it there. Maybe he wasn't always honest, but he'd just told her three lifetimes' worth of truth and there wasn't much else he could say. He held his breath.

"This is your way to win the bet, isn't it?"

He slammed his hand down on the table, surprising them both.

"Damn it, Jessica. I don't care about the lousy bet.

Yes, I want you. Does it matter if I win or lose? Hell, no. We can even pretend I lose. Make love to me, Jessica, and I'll still do whatever you want."

She rolled her chair back against the window, as far as she could go. "You are such a guy, spouting that 'I want you. Oh, baby, I need you' nonsense. I can't do that. I have absolutely no reason to trust you. None. Zilch. Nada. Am I attracted to you? *In spades.* Does that mean I'm just going to let you screw my brains out? Read my lips. *No way.*"

He was dying to touch her, but she really didn't look like she wanted to be touched right now. Instead, he stared at his hands, a farmer's hands in a tailored suit. He thought for a long time before speaking. "I want more from you than that, Jessica."

"I wish I could believe you, but you scare the smarts out of me, Adam." Her voice softened at the end. He heard her fear and her need and he began to hope.

"Let me prove it to you. Go out to lunch with me. Lunch. Not dinner. Not drinks. Just lunch. We'll come back here and you go back to your office, I go back to mine. No harm, no foul, no sex."

She looked at him with interest. That was progress. "Lunch?"

Their gazes locked until finally he looked away. He wanted so badly to see trust in her eyes, yet every time it started to glimmer he felt like the weasel that he was. "I just like talking to you, Jess. I spend days by myself and I'm just not that good a conversationalist, you know?"

She crossed her arms across her chest, seeing right through him. "Words are not your problem."

He didn't give up, though. He couldn't give up. "You'll come with me?"

"Just stamp 'Sucker' on my forehead."

Adam looked around, checked that no one was watching through the glass, then leaned over her desk and kissed her. "You won't regret this, Jessica. I swear. I'm going to be the best thing that ever happened to you."

He made that promise to himself as well.

Jessica didn't look happy at all. "Yeah, that's what I'm afraid of."

JESSICA SAYS: "You there?"

Mickey says: "No."

Jessica says: "You're supposed to be my friend."

Mickey says: "And you're damned lucky I am. Most people wouldn't put up with your neuroses."

Jessica says (whispering): "He's taking me to lunch."

Mickey says: "Why are you even fighting this? Go do him. Get it out of your system. You're driving us all NUTS!"

Jessica says (inserting a cute picture of a squirrel): "He's saying all the right things, M. Remind me that he is the enemy. Remind me that I only have two more years before I can afford the Porsche. I'm...getting... weaker...."

Mickey says (inserting pornographic cartoon clip art): "Forget the Porsche."

Jessica says (regretfully): "We're only going to lunch."

Mickey says: "What time are you going to be back?"

Jessica says (whispering again): "A couple of hours. I have a meeting at three."

Mickey says (because she is the truest sort of friend): "I'll be online. Don't forget your tissues."

HE TOOK HER to a small French place in the suburbs north of town. It was one of those places couples went when they didn't want to be seen, and she immediately wondered how he knew about it. Their table was in the back room, a fire burning in the large stone fireplace that ran along the entire back wall. A row of rustic, wood-framed windows lined the side wall, looking out over the garden terrace that reminded Jessica of one of those villas in Tuscany. Flowerpots overflowing with color were artfully placed here and there, and grapevines rose up the stone pillars, weaving their way in and out of the wooden lattice-work overhead. Amazing what a good landscape architect could do with the right tools, she thought to herself.

The setting was fitting because the whole lunch was like a dream. Adam held her chair, he kept her water glass filled—wine was definitely *out*—and in general, made sure that everything was perfect.

And damn it all, it was.

"Do you think this place does catering?" she asked,

trying to a) make light conversation, b) avoid the bold look in his eyes and c) possibly find a sumptuous caterer for her mother's birthday party, all at the same time. Efficiency, thy name is woman.

"Planning a party?" he asked, completely unaware of her hidden talents. Although it wasn't as if he would ever appreciate such things anyway.

"It's a surprise party for my mother's birthday."

He frowned, an appealing frown, and she wondered if he did anything badly. So far, other than the "he wants to get rid of my position" thing, he seemed pretty darn near perfect. "You don't want to cook?" he asked, which, she was delighted to note, wasn't a darn near perfect question.

"I don't cook," she said, sniffing.

Again the frown, a little darker this time. "At all?"

Jessica waved a careless hand in the air. "No. No time."

"Oh."

Such a wealth of meaning in that one syllable. Over her years of singledom, she had learned a little about deciphering male tone. "Do you?" she asked, determined to put this ball firmly back in his court—right where it belonged.

"Some. My mom taught me how when I was a kid."

Okay, he was redeemed. Somewhat. "So what do you do with your laundry? Self-serve or full-serve? I bet you just pay for it." Under the table, she crossed her fingers.

"Why is that? You don't think I know how to do my own laundry?" He looked insulted. "Of course I can."

"My father never did laundry," she said, fake-casually studying her nails.

In true consultant mode, he dodged the opportunity for self-incrimination and—typical—asked a question. "You go self-serve or full-serve?"

"I do my own," she said, not mentioning that she usually took it to her parents' house to save money. Seemed silly to waste all those quarters when there was a perfectly comfortable place to watch TV, eat and, best of all, use the washer and dryer for free.

"That's good," he said, nodding in a mysterious considering manner, his eyes vague.

"Why?"

His gaze refocused on her. "I don't know. Self-sufficiency is important, I suppose."

Jessica laughed, half in relief, and quickly changed the conversation to something that didn't make her look bad or sneeze. "So do you have an apartment back in Alabama? Where do you keep your stuff?"

"I have a house."

She picked up her water glass, then put it down again. "No kidding? I wouldn't have pegged you for the house type."

"And what is the house type?"

"You know, married, mowing the lawn, fixing leaky faucets." An awful thought occurred to her. "Oh, my God. You're married, aren't you?"

An older lady turned around at the table next to

them and fixed Jessica with a disapproving glare. Jessica slunk down in her seat.

Adam just rolled his eyes, which pleased her because, if he was really married, he would have been mad, not frustrated. A definite sign. "I'm not married," he said tightly.

Relieved beyond measure, Jessica beamed at him. "I believe you."

"Good," he said, with a crooked smile. Her glance touched on his mouth, and she remembered his kiss. All at once, the room began to heat, and memories turned to want. She could feel the warmth in her blood, delicious waves of desire lapping between her thighs. What was it about the things that were bad for you? Why did they have to be so damn tasty?

"Jessica," he said, a low warning in his voice, but his eyes betrayed him.

Silently the waiter came and cleared the table and the moment was gone. After he had left, Jessica balanced her chin in her palm. Interested, attentive, intellectual. All in all, it was a great move. "So why the house, then? Is it a family home?"

"No. Someday it's gonna be, though. I want a house with noise and laughter," he said, not looking at her, looking down into his crystal water glass at a dream of the home he'd never had. Jessica thought about her own home, yelling and fighting and tears—but underneath all the noise and agitation lay a rock-hard foundation of love. It seemed that she'd been lucky.

When she studied his face, she saw the vulnerability

that lay hidden beneath the strength. Usually he kept it so well hidden. "You missed out on that whole noise and laughter thing, huh?"

Then he looked at her and blinked and the vulnerability was gone. "Oh, no. I had a great family, a great childhood, no dysfunction or abuse or anything. We were just always working. In the fields, taking care of the cows."

No way. "You really had cows?" If it had been anybody but the farm boy, she would have thought they were pulling one over on her, but when he left the consultant mask at home, she trusted him—which was scary in itself, considering who he was.

He smiled at her, looking a little embarrassed. "Just four or five at any one time."

"Wow," was all she could say. "Do you have cows now?" she asked, just as the waiter appeared with the check. The stodgy old guy shot her a weird look. Jessica shot him one back.

Adam gave the guy his credit card and then laughed. "Oh, no. The house is an old Victorian place in the middle of town."

A definite fixer-upper, she thought to herself. Major work.

"Sounds great," was what she said.

"I bet you'd like it. It needs some work. I do some painting and repairs when I'm home."

Jessica had begun thinking of contractors and painters and mentally tallying price tags, then she realized he meant to do it himself. "You can do everything, can't you?"

"Uh, yeah. I'm a superhero. Did I not mention that? And no, I can't do everything. I just try and figure out what's important to me. What do *you* want to do with your life? You know, when you turn seventy and look back on your accomplishments, what are you going to be proud of? Surely it's not just your job."

Her laughter was just a little forced. "Obviously career is not a big issue in your family."

He cocked his head and studied her. "And it is in yours?"

"I'm the first Barnes kid to go to college, and I'm going to be the first Barnes vice president, too. I'd like to be the first Barnes to own a Porsche, but I've been thinking about that some, and maybe that's just greed. I'd be willing to give up the Porsche," she said, even though secretly she wasn't willing to give up her dream yet.

"It's just a car."

Spoken like a man who parked one in his garage. "Oh yeah, and a diamond is just a rock."

Smoothly he slipped back into consultant mode. She was learning to recognize the passive, expressionless face. "You never answered my question."

"What would I be proud of?" Jessica repeated, shaking her head. "I don't know."

"What about a family, kids?"

She waved a hand. "Yeah. Someday."

The veneer slipped a little. "You shouldn't just dismiss that."

Mr. Closet Chauvinist was starting to piss her off, probably because she knew it was true, had absolutely no control over it, and it frightened her like hell. "I'm not going to hear a lecture from you on the ticking clock."

He picked up her poorly hidden anger pretty well, again scoring good points. Jessica knew because she was keeping score. He took her hand, sending a warm shiver through her body.

"Nah, that's not what I'm trying to say. What if what we think we're supposed to be isn't really what we're supposed to be?"

The feeling of skin against skin was beginning to seduce her into mindless oblivion, but she climbed through the depths of the silky waters and fought for air. "Let's stop talking in abstracts. Bring this to a personal level. Are you talking about me or you?"

His thumb stroked her palm, and he talked lucidly, intelligently, completely unaware of how she was melting into goo. "Well, you. Look at it this way. You've decided that you're destined to be a corporate vice president, your family is proud of you, great success, blah, blah, blah. But...what if that's not what you're destined to be? What if your success lies somewhere else and you just don't know it?"

The world shifted on its axis. Jessica slipped her hand free and had to hold tightly to the chair arms.

"I'm not going to make it, am I? My job is toast, isn't it?"

He smiled, even white teeth, a smile meant to calm and soothe. "Jessica, in this day and age, people change jobs like changing toothbrushes. You can't stay there forever."

"I'm good at what I do," she said, not wanting to discuss changing jobs. Not with him. Stubbornly, she pushed the thoughts aside.

"You're great at what you do, but don't you ever think about the unknown, the untried? What are you missing because you're so determined to make it in the business world? You're smart and creative and so full of energy. You'd be successful at whatever you decide to do."

Flattery. The oldest trick in the book for a good reason. It always worked. Somewhat mollified, she leaned back in her chair and folded her arms across her chest. It was a lucky thing he'd never seen her high-school years, or he wouldn't have been so certain. "You're good."

He looked slightly insulted. "I meant that."

And she hadn't meant to hurt him. Instead, she put her hand on the table, hoping that he'd pick it up again. "I know. Maybe when I'm retired I'll take up painting."

In typical male, oblivious fashion, he ignored her hand. "You shouldn't put off your dreams, Jessica."

Dreams. When he looked at her like that, when she lost herself in his gray-green eyes full of promises, he could seduce her into anything. Seduce her into thinking her dreams didn't involve a vice presidency, but instead lay down some primrose path strewn with lace curtains and chocolate chip cookies.

Two days ago, she would have been shocked even to be considering a future outside Hard-Wire. Now she was having trouble imagining a future outside Adam.

Regrettably, lunch had to end. Work was calling.

He walked her back to the car and when he put the keys in the ignition, instead of starting the car, he sat in silence, staring at the steering column. Finally, he turned to her. "Thank you for coming with me," he said, the hint of warm Southern winds seeping into his voice.

"It was my pleasure."

"Could I see you tonight?"

It would be so easy to tell him yes, to forget all the other responsibilities and just live life, but Jessica had spent too many years learning how to get ahead, learning how to overcome her weaknesses, just to throw it all away. "I've got to start coaching tonight. It's the first practice."

"Do you need help?"

He was scoring big points here. Big, big points. "Sure," she said with a not-a-big-deal shrug. "You'd do that?"

Adam answered with a not-a-big-deal shrug of his own. "Why not?"

"I'll forward the note from Delia. She included a little map."

There was a long moment of awkward silence. They should be going back to work soon. She knew that, he knew that, but both of them sat, staring straight ahead, not willing to go just yet.

His hands tightened on the steering wheel. "Would you mind if I kissed you?"

"Excuse me?" she said, knowing she had heard the words right, but wanting to hear them again, just so she could memorize everything, get all the details right.

"Now. Earlier I told you that lunch would be no harm, no foul, no sex, and I'm working real hard to keep my promise, but I need to kiss you. I need to kiss you bad."

When he got that spark in his eyes, that bit of desperation that was so unlike him, she could never tell him no.

Masterfully she restrained herself from launching into his arms. "I suppose it wouldn't be breaking any rules, and I did tell you that foreplay was acceptable." She pretended to consider it further. "All right."

Slowly he leaned forward. "I'm glad you said that."

Then he kissed her. At the touch of his lips, her lashes drifted shut, and she lost all thought in the warm, sensual feelings that he stirred in her. It was just like in her dreams as he traced a line down her neck, tasting her flesh in some erotic feast.

His teeth scraped the lobe of her ear, and she

gasped, needing support and finding none. He did that to her, made her walk a wire without any safety net at all. Against her skin she felt his breath, warm and ragged, and it pleased her. She wasn't the only one who was missing the safety net.

The soft leather seat was a poor substitute for him and she twisted first one way then the other, sinking closer to the tantalizing rhythm that was building between her legs.

Still it wasn't enough. She wanted him closer, wanted to bring this torture to an end, but he seemed determined to tease her, each new touch of his lips driving her further and further out of control. He made it so easy to forget things—important things, but right at the moment, the most important thing was the taste of his mouth, and the way he touched her, his hands finding places that made her burn.

Wanting more, she wrapped her arms around his neck, moving closer until her aching breasts rubbed against him, salving herself with the heat of his skin.

She heard his tortured groan and smiled in triumph. To punish her or to tease her—she didn't know which—he nipped at her throat, the sharp sting turning her on even more. Never had kissing made her so fabulously voracious.

It was heady and intoxicating and more satisfying than any victory she'd ever known.

Now his mouth returned to hers and his tongue slipped between her lips, exploring and seducing. Against her heart, she felt the uneven rise and fall of his chest, his reaction to her. He was stripped of his polish and his control, a strong combination of man and lust left behind.

And for this instant he was hers. Jessica buried her hands in his hair, keeping him anchored, giving as much as she received. She traced the outline of his lips with her tongue, a move she'd never made before, but today, with Adam, she wanted to slip even further beneath the veneer, Delilah to his Samson. Make him reckless and wild. Like her.

She didn't have long to wait. His hands slipped roughly beneath her, lifting her, kneading the flesh of her bottom, and her hips pumped blindly in answer. Her blood throbbed like a pulse between her legs. All the will in her dissolved and she felt herself mold to his form. All traces of steel were gone; instead she was pure liquid.

She had wanted to be the conqueror, instead she was the vanquished. But for the life of her, she couldn't stop, wouldn't stop.

As if he sensed her weakness, his hand moved beneath her skirt, tracing the damp nylon of her panties, and instinctively her thighs clenched tight, locking him there.

His body froze, and her eyes flew open.

He still didn't move.

She waited, stared into his eyes and felt one hundred-and-eighty degrees of pure green fire burning in her direction. She was going to die, the first woman ever to die from repressed sexual frustration.

"Jessica, you've got a choice here. We either go home—your apartment, my hotel, the Sears Tower, location's not an issue—right now and finish this, no foreplay just full penetration," he took a long rasping breath. "Or we go back to the office, and I'm not going to lay a hand on you again until both my sanity and my control return."

Right then it occurred to her what he was doing. The bet. This was her chance to tell him to drive back to the city, tell him to cool his jets and wait another eight days, another eight days of one-hundred-percent guaranteed, thigh-clenching, heart-thumping, blood-pressure-reeling torture. Another eight days to victory.

Or an easy fifteen-minute sprint to defeat. Mind-blowing, ear-popping, wave-crashing defeat.

Victory or defeat? Her body was still on fire from his touch, every inch of her crying to be touched again. Defeat would never be so sweet.

He would lay her down on her bed, and she would watch as every inch of his marvelous flesh was exposed, and after that...yes, right there.

Afterward, she would lie in the afterglow of defeat, happily sated.

But then Jessica sneezed. And because God had a marvelous sense of humor, she sneezed again.

At that moment she hated every overly hormonal-teenage boy who had ever ignored her, hated every perky cheerleader who was probably living a perfectly normal perky life, hated every pompous teacher who had ever sneered when she'd shouted out the wrong answer—hated them all.

Because Jessica Barnes didn't have it in her to lose.

Slowly she removed one hand from his shoulder, then the other. She straightened in her seat, until his hands were no longer touching her, no longer bringing her tidal waves of pleasure. Now she was just cold.

If he had been more of a weasel, he would have tried to talk her out of leaving. He could have seduced her right into his bed, and they both knew it. And Jessica knew that exactly eight days from now—well, seven days and eleven hours—she was going to make sure he knew exactly what a victory dance entailed.

She'd never met a man who knew exactly how much she needed to win, and she was willing to forgive a whole lot of Adam's sins just because he knew.

They didn't talk. Adam turned on the stereo, playing some electric guitar, blues-music thing that was actually much better than Jessica had thought it would be.

She leaned back in the warmth of the seat, listened to the hum of the 320-horsepower engine, and began to think that maybe, just maybe, she could have it all.

Including Adam.

8

JESSICA SAYS: "You there?"

Mickey says: "Of course. Tell me all about it."

Jessica says: "I think I'm either in serious love or lust."

Mickey says: "Does either one mean you got laid?"

Jessica says (checking to see if anyone is looking over her shoulder): "No."

Mickey says: "Why?"

Jessica says (with a fragile sigh): "Because he's a gentleman."

Mickey says (while playing bad violins in the background): "I'm going to hear all the details, aren't I?"

Jessica says: "We went to this cool French restaurant. Out in Arlington Heights. *Très* secluded."

Mickey says: "And?"

Jessica says: "We had lunch."

Mickey says (with increasing frustration): "And?"

Jessica says: "I had dessert."

Mickey says (beating her head against the desk): "I'm going to go defuse matter. Excuse me."

Jessica says: "Mickey?"

Jessica says: "Mick?"

Jessica says (yelling so as to be heard in four states): "*Mickey!*"

Mickey says (having now safely diffused matter and feeling much more relaxed): "Yes?"

Jessica says: "We made out in his car."

Mickey says: "Made out? That is so seventies."

Jessica merely laughs: "Hehehe."

Mickey says: Meaningful silence.

Jessica says (not quite so cocky): "You're coming tonight, right?"

Mickey says (looking longingly at the latest intern and realizing he was in elementary school when she was in junior high, and although she hasn't had sex in eleven months, fourteen days and about three hours, she isn't that pathetic. At least not yet.): "Probably not."

Jessica says (desperate): "Why *not?*"

Mickey says (watching intern walk away): "Oh, sorry, misunderstood."

Jessica says (in a needy female voice): "Adam's going to be there."

Mickey says (with steel in her voice): "I'm definitely *not* coming."

Jessica says: "I want you to meet him. See what you think. It's v. important for my friends to approve."

Mickey says: "Why? You're going to go to bed with him anyway. Odds are running fourteen to one in his favor."

Jessica says (puzzled): "How'd you get that?"

Mickey says (pulling out PalmPilot): "Cassandra:

$40—Adam. Beth: $10—Jessica. Mickey: $100—Adam. It's pretty much a sure thing."

Jessica says (sniffing): "I have to win the bet."

Mickey says (in a worldly manner): "Of all the start-ups in all the towns in all the world, he walks into yours. Even Bogie lost, J. It's not a crime."

Jessica says (pitifully): "It's the first time in my life I've actually wanted to lose."

Mickey says (beating head against desk, v. Charlie Brown): "AAGGGHHH!"

Jessica says (after politely waiting until beating is done): "So does that mean you'll be there tonight?"

Mickey says (with a last yearning look at the studmo intern): "Only because I don't have anything better to do."

Jessica says (thinking her friends are the best): "Cool."

IT SHOULDN'T have surprised him that Jessica had managed to move the practice from a little field in Roseland to the track at the University of Chicago, but he was still impressed. The track would be better for the team, but traffic getting in and out of the campus was a bear.

After work, Adam had gone back to the hotel, changed into sweats and a T-shirt, and loaded up the water and oranges that Jessica had charged him with bringing. He was interested in seeing how she'd be with the girls. All afternoon she had been buried in her office, doing research on how to coach. He had to hand it to her, Jessica didn't do anything half-measure. That's what he admired about her.

Just as he turned on to 55th Street, his cell phone rang and he answered.

"Taylor."

"Adam? This is Brittany Morgan."

He searched his memory for the name, but couldn't come up with a face. Disappointment sneaked up on him, disappointment because he had hoped to hear Jessica's voice on the line. "Hello, Brittany. Glad to hear from you. What can I do for you?" Adam found a parking space along the street and wheeled in.

"Listen, I know I'm being forward, but since you aren't going to be in town much longer—" How had she known that? He racked his brain trying to remember who he'd told. "—I didn't want to wait. I was wondering if you were free for dinner on Friday night."

Patiently, he drummed his fingers on the steering wheel, figuring she was a book club prospect, but couldn't pin her down. Not that it really mattered. He cut the ignition. "Brittany, you can't know how much it means to me that you've asked me. I'm really flattered, but I have to be honest with you, I just started a relationship with a woman and it feels right. In fact, if anything, I'm terrified of screwing it up."

"Oh."

Whenever a female was reduced to one syllable, it was bad. Adam quickly backtracked.

"You know, there's this one guy I work with who I

think would be perfect for you. Maybe I could give him your number?"

"I suppose that would be okay. Is he as nice as you?"

Translation: Is he gainfully employed? "Oh, yeah. A real straight arrow and a frequent-flier jockey just like me. Just the other day he was moaning because he hadn't met any nice women since he'd been in town. This way, I'll be doing him a favor."

"That'd be nice." She gave him her phone number and he wrote it down in his PDA.

"You take care, Brittany."

"Thank you. And Adam, I hope everything works out for you with the—lady."

"Yeah."

He hung up the phone and waited patiently. Ten minutes had passed before he realized that his con-science—and he firmly believed it was *only* his con-science that caused the conversations in his head—was staying quiet. He didn't know if that meant he was doing the right thing or the wrong thing, but he supposed that this time his mother wasn't going to swoop down and bop him on the head. And he wasn't fool enough to miss it, either.

Instead, he got out, unloaded the cooler, and made his way to the field. Jessica was already there, wearing some tight red stretch pants that sent all his blood down south of the Mason-Dixon line. She looked up and waved, a coach's whistle in hand, and he felt the silliest urge to wave back. The adult male in him overcame the goofy kid and instead he just smiled.

"Adam, I've got some people I want you to meet. First off, girls, this is Adam Taylor, he's going to help me coach. I've seen him run and he's fast—" she shot him a pointed look "—very fast."

"Adam, this is Sonya, Christine, Jasmine and Latrice."

From behind her, a tall brunette cleared her throat. Jessica smiled. "And this is Mickey."

Mickey studied him from behind oval tortoiseshell glasses, making him more than a little nervous. He recognized her from Charles's wedding, and knew that she was friends with Annie and Jessica, but that's all he knew about her.

He smiled and stuck out his hand. "Pleased to meet you, Mickey. I've heard a lot of really nice things about you," he said.

Translation: I haven't heard anything at all, but I know you're a good friend of Jessica's, so I'm going to suck up big-time here.

Immediately Mickey shot a frowning look to Jessica, who shrugged.

"From Charles. Charles has told me a lot of nice things about you," he corrected.

She didn't look convinced, so he opted to turn his attention back to Jessica. It seemed safer. "The floor's all yours, Coach."

Jessica stepped forward and turned into Vince Lombardi. For fifteen minutes, she gave the girls a lecture on the proper attitude of an athlete. The shorter girl with pigtails—Jasmine—began to fiddle with her shoelaces. Sonya was drawing pictures in the dirt. Christine and Latrice were taking it all in, smiling at the right times, but whether Jessica realized it or not, she had lost fifty percent of her audience. Not good for Day One.

"Who's heard of Jesse Owens? Raise your hands."

All hands stayed firmly on deck.

"Well, that's not important. He ran the hundred-meter dash in the 1936 Olympics and went on to win four gold medals. Do you know what he said?"

The girls stared at her blankly.

"He said, 'If you don't try to win, you might as well hold the Olympics in somebody's backyard.' And that's what we're going to do girls—try to win. But we're not going to just try. Each one of you has the potential to go all the way. To win, and win big."

"Do we get to start running yet?" Christine asked. "My momma is going to be back to pick me up in an hour." She got to her feet, and started stretching.

"Start running? Nay. Girls, today we are going to fly." Jessica blew on her whistle, three sharp blasts. "Line up and we'll do one time around the track. I want to clock each one of you and see exactly how much work we have to do."

The girls took off, Christine and Latrice sped along in fits and starts, but overall, they were solid athletes. Jasmine found her own pace and Sonya, well, Sonya seemed content to move a little slower.

Jessica took off after Sonya, a determined look on her face, and Adam took the time to score extra Brownie points with Mickey.

He put on his consultant's smile. "So, do you run?"

"No."

Obviously Mickey wasn't the outgoing type. Adam was going to have to wing it on his own. "What do you do?"

"I'm an astrophysicist."

He studied her, trying to determine if that was a joke. Judging from the way her wide mouth was pressed into one single tight line, he didn't think so. Better to err on the side of caution than to piss off Jessica's friend and possibly ruin a potential ally forever.

"You do defense work or commercial avionics?" he said, pulling from the little he knew from going to lunch with the suits in the government verticals.

"Commercial. I don't believe in death."

"Yeah, makes me a little uncomfortable myself." He watched as Jessica gestured in a grand fashion to Sonya, who looked a little mystified. "You think she needs help?"

Mickey just laughed, and for the first time she softened up. "Are you kidding? Jessica stayed up all last night going over her notes for today. I'd actually be afraid to help, might screw up the grand plan."

"Have you known her a long time?"

"About ten years. We were roommates in college. I've known her a lot longer than you."

Adam didn't miss the barb. "It doesn't take long to make up your mind about Jessica."

"Have you?" she said, arching one eyebrow over the rim of her glasses.

Adam feigned typical male ignorance. "Have I what?"

"Made up your mind about J."

He watched as Jessica worked with Sonya, coaxing her into a run, and the way her smile seemed to touch the girl. Yeah, he'd made up his mind. Some things were just too difficult to fight. Adam nodded.

That seemed to satisfy Mickey and she crossed her arms over her chest. "You going to leave soon? Jessica says you're out of Alabama."

"The contract will be up in about a month."

"But you're going to leave?" she continued, making him spell things out.

Leaving only made him think of home—his rambling house in DeKalb County. He thought of the way the afternoon sun peeked through the mountains and lit up the old hardwood floors. Then he thought of Jessica waiting for him when he got home from the road and he swallowed, willing fluid to his dry mouth. "Yeah."

"If you hurt her, I'll have someone come and break your legs."

He shook off his fantasy life and met her eyes, tough and protective. "Huh?"

"I've got some very big connections, Mr. Taylor.

Never underestimate a woman who plays with radioactivity for a living."

"I've learned the hard way never to underestimate a woman. Any woman. Doesn't matter what she does for a living."

"Yeah, that's all well and good, but I meant what I said."

"Message received," Adam replied easily, but that didn't mean he didn't feel his conscience pricking at his gut. Wanting to end this conversation, he looked at his watch. Half an hour had passed.

Now Jessica had the girls doing stretches and squats, their faces flushed and sweating. Adam picked up the cooler because he didn't think that Jessica was ready to release them just yet, and he didn't think the dominatrix was going to come to the refreshments, so the refreshments were going to have to go to the dominatrix.

He laughed to himself and donned the imaginary white hat. Time to call in the cavalry. And just for today, that was Adam.

JESSICA LOOKED UP from the exercises to see Mickey walking over, Adam right behind her hefting the cooler easily on one shoulder. She stopped in midstretch, admiring a man in his natural environment— manual labor.

And not just any man—Adam.

Sonya pulled impatiently at her T-shirt. "Coach, can we quit for a minute?"

Jessica studied the round face, the sweet, innocent eyes and, against her better judgment, nodded. "Just for a minute, Sonya. What are we here for?"

"To run."

"No, we're here to win, and in order to do that, we've got to work longer and harder than anyone else."

Sonya stared at her blankly, and Jessica sighed. There were five more weeks before their first meet, so there was still time.

"Who wants some water?" asked Adam, instantly the hero as all four girls ran to him, shouting, "Me, me, me!"

Knowing she was beaten, Jessica shook her head, lifted a bottle from the cooler, and then drank heavily. It was good. "Thanks."

"No problem. What time is yard exercise over?"

Today he must have left his competitive spirit at home. Jessica flashed him a fake smile. "Very funny. Another fifteen minutes. We'll do two more sprints and then call it a day." She turned to her girls proudly. "We've made great progress."

"Make sure you drink lots of water," Mickey said while handing out oranges to everyone. "Your blood pressure may drop as you exercise. The water from your sweat reduces the amount of water in your blood plasma and you've got to keep up your fluid intake, or you may get dizzy or nauseous or even faint."

Christine nodded. "I nearly fainted once."

Mickey sat down on the grass beside her. "Did you get dehydrated?"

"No. My brother put a frog in my room."

"I see."

"My mother yelled and yelled at him and said that if he didn't take it outside right away, that I would faint."

"And did you?"

"No, he took it outside and I just watched some more TV."

"But you could've fainted, couldn't you?"

Christine nodded most emphatically.

Jessica watched as Adam tied Latrice's shoelaces and cut up another orange for Jasmine. He was patient and seemed to work much better with the girls than Jessica did. Someday he would make a great father.

She was glad that he had come out to help her. The team needed all the help it could get. Christine and Latrice were natural runners, with long legs and a great stride. Jasmine and Sonya were going to take some work, but they had a great attitude and Jessica knew that with the proper amount of training, they could win the meet.

After the break, they went back to practice, two more sprints, just as Jessica had said, and then the parents arrived to pick up the girls. Jessica explained to each mother the importance of proper diet and rest, and showed them how they could practice with their child at home.

When the last car had driven away, she gave

Mickey a high five, then sat down on the wooden benches and relaxed for the first time in twenty-four hours.

"You did good, J."

Jessica smiled. Yeah, she had. "We're going to win. They're great kids. I can feel it."

"You know, they're really just here to learn about training and competing. I'm not sure that it's that important for them actually to win," said Adam.

"Obviously you have never suffered the agony of defeat."

"I'm siding with Adam on this, Jess. Don't work them so hard."

"Why?"

"Because they're kids."

"I'm disappointed in both of you. These kids are going to face a lot of things in life and I'm trying to teach them how to level the playing field. Something to help them in the real world."

"Jess, they're just kids."

"Do you think kids can't be mean and brutal? You lived a sheltered life, didn't you?"

"Jess—" Adam touched her on the arm "—it's just a game."

"No, you don't understand. I'm the coach here. We do things my way. If you don't like it, find your own team. But you'll see—both of you—when the meet is done, these girls are going to walk away with their heads high, because they have triumphed over adversity."

Mickey knew when to quit. "Well, I need to be heading home. Got a hot date with my DVD player and possibly a glass of wine."

Jessica stared at Mickey, hard, using mental telepathy to tell her that wasn't what she had planned. "I thought we could all go out to dinner, or maybe get a drink somewhere?"

"The three of us?" Mickey, completely missing out on the mental telepathy, looked shocked.

Jessica frowned. "Well, yes."

Adam interrupted. "Jessica, why don't we not worry about this tonight? I know some guys at Kearney, Markham and Williams, and I think I know just the guy for Mickey. Pete O'Connell. We'll go out together. The four of us."

Mickey looked satisfied. She picked up her backpack. As she headed off across the field, she yelled over her shoulder, "See ya later, J. Nice to meet you, Adam."

Jessica watched her friend leave, more than a little peeved. "I didn't think it was that crazy."

Adam put his arm around her and they sat that way for a bit. "You can't keep your life exactly the way you want it, Jessica."

"Well, maybe not, but with proper hard work and initiative, I can at least maintain some semblance of normalcy."

He planted a kiss in her hair. "We should go."

Jessica sighed. "I've got to take a shower."

"Need a hand there, little lady?" he asked in a John Wayne voice with wicked, wicked eyes.

Suddenly she didn't feel sweaty and sticky and grungy. Thoughts of a long, hot shower with Adam had her feeling...a little randy. "I don't think you'd survive."

He smiled, shaking his head. "I suppose this means another bet."

"No. Same rules."

Adam leaned closer, his smile deepening. "Foreplay is allowed?"

"Yeah. Foreplay's allowed."

He stroked his chin, his gaze wandering down her body, then slowly wandering back up, sending long rivers of heat from her head to her toes, and swirling in a couple of hot spots in between. When he met her eyes, she shivered. "You're toast, Barnes."

"Bend me, tease me," she sang, loving the way his eyes flared with desire.

Adam lifted the cooler onto his shoulder, and held out a hand. "Let's go."

Before he got out of hand-range, she reached out and pinched him—just once—right on that marvelous ass, just to let him know that she thought he was cute.

He turned, nearly dropping the cooler, and she winked at him, shrugging apologetically.

And there, right on the forty-yard line of Amos Alonzo Stagg Field, with the last bits of sun shining down on him, he blushed.

Jessica sighed. She was in love.

ADAM FOLLOWED her home, driving in a lust-filled haze. Even the usual traffic jams on the Eisenhower couldn't break his mood. For the first time in a long, long while, he felt marvelously alive. The last lines of sun beat down across his arms, warm on his skin as he hummed softly to the music on the CD.

He kept her taillights in sight, but just before her exit, she punched the accelerator, and he was stuck behind an eighteen-wheeler.

But today he was in too good a mood to let it worry him. Another fifteen minutes and he found himself at her apartment door. A door that was slightly ajar.

He poked his head inside and began to smile.

The first thing he saw was a streak of red nylon— her pants—placed strategically across the back of her couch. He closed his eyes, his own little *Penthouse* movie jump-starting in his head. A pair of shoes and socks had been kicked off right near the back wall. At the beginning of the hallway, he picked up the white T-shirt she had been wearing, and just as he was about to call out, he heard the sound of water running.

Jessica had turned on the shower.

So little Miss Barnes was playing games. Well, that was fine with him. Humming under his breath, he ventured further and spied her sports bra hanging from the doorknob of the bathroom.

He took the flimsy piece of cotton and shot it, rubber-band style, into her bedroom. He twisted the knob and walked into the confines of the small room.

She had one of those glass shower enclosures, but

the humidity had steamed up the room, making anything impossible to see except for a long, golden line of skin.

With efficient movements, Adam stripped down and stepped inside.

Immediately he forgot to breathe. He had imagined Jessica so many times in his fantasies that she had seemed almost unreal. Water cascaded down her body, following the line of her breasts, around the curve of her stomach, and then down to collect in the dark curls between her legs.

Never had a woman affected him like this. It was like an obsession, his body intent on possessing her, his mind focused on knowing her, his eyes drawn to her, memorizing the compact lines of her form, caressing the gentle arc of her breasts. At this moment, all he could imagine was touching her. Just one touch.

His hands ached simply to brush across her flesh, but he was afraid, afraid that if he did, she would disappear.

She peered up at him through spiked lashes, blinking several times. Her hair was drenched, the water coloring it to a dark brown, and causing it to cling tightly to her face.

"Adam?"

The sound of her voice was enough. He took the bar of soap from her hand and began to wash her. The soft, flowery scent of the soap filled the air, an oddly feminine choice for Jessica, but as his gaze caressed her body once again, he marveled at how completely small and feminine she was.

Almost reverently, he knelt before her, picked up one foot in his hands, and glided the bar over her smooth skin. Drops of water slid down her body, glistening in the light. He ministered first to one foot, then the other. Rubbing, massaging, cleaning. His hands moved up to her calves, using strong strokes to soothe her muscles. With a long sigh, she leaned back against the shower wall in silent invitation.

Upward he moved, his hands lathering her firm thighs, his thumbs circling in place, digging deep into the taut muscles. Her legs parted, a gesture of both trust and desire, and he took one long shuddering breath.

He stood and turned her so that she faced the tiled wall, and began to soap her back, her shoulders, the smooth skin of her buttocks. He moved to stand behind her, sheltering her body with his own. The spray of water ran between them, and his hands curved around her rib cage to cup her breasts.

His body began to throb, demanding release, and he worried that he wouldn't keep his word. And then she turned, her arms curving around his neck, and she brought his head down for a kiss.

Adam pulled her closer, and at the taste of her mouth, he pushed his worries aside. Tonight was for her, and as she'd said, foreplay was allowed.

9

JESSICA SIGHED with pleasure, pure bliss running across her skin. The water was hot and seductive, and Adam's hard body pressed against her as if they belonged together. That was the way he made her feel. They were two completely different people, from two different places in their lives, and yet she *knew* him. His mind, his heart, and his hundred-percent-satisfaction-guaranteed body.

She'd seen him in suits, she'd seen him in shorts, but never, *never*, had a man looked better wearing nothing but water.

Everything about him was pure muscle. A chest that was fortunately, yet still regrettably, more than twice the size of hers. Lean hips, a derriere beyond compare and, well, she felt a little shy eyeing his erection with such—uh, hum—greed, but holy cow.

Tonight the Cubbies were going to the World Series.

His tongue swept into her mouth, thrusting and circling and she forgot about the Cubs, forgot about baseball. God, the man could kiss. She answered him back, getting amazingly turned on by the feel of kissing him in the nude.

For not long enough, she held on to him. Wanting to stay like this forever.

Adam had other ideas. He pressed her back against the wall, taking one nipple into his mouth. Quietly, she moaned, feeling the tingle between her legs change to something more insistent. She buried her hands in his hair, letting the water stream over her fingers as he pulled and suckled. With each draw of his mouth, he went harder. Against his shoulders, she fisted and unfisted her hands, her breasts growing heavy and full.

His hands were so big, they spanned her waist, and went lower, cupping her rear, parting her thighs.

Her hips rubbed against his erection, needing to release the pressure inside her, and he laughed. Low, wicked.

She wanted to scream.

But he must have sensed her need, because one finger slid inside her and instantly she pressed against it—hard.

Slowly he moved, in and out, and her hips followed.

He began to circle and stroke her, back and forth, his eyes darkening to green as he watched her. Her lashes drifted shut and he moved her forward, letting the stream of water rush down her. She gasped as the delicious pressure ran over her sensitized nipples. Her back arched, moving closer to his hand, his magical hand.

Her orgasm came closer, just out of her reach. To

her horror, he took his hand away and she groaned in frustration.

But he wasn't finished. He knelt before her and lifted her leg over his shoulder, and then his mouth touched her. His lips surrounded her, with the same hard pressure as before, and she leaned forward, needing the support of his shoulders and head to stay upright. His tongue stroked and lashed, just enough to have her hips bucking against him, but his hands held her tight, her moans increasing in an embarrassing amount as each wave of pleasure crested higher and higher.

The lights in the shower began to glow, the world disappearing as only the pulse between her legs seized control. Quick gasps escaped from her lips as her orgasm rose closer and closer to the surface. Her muscles began to shake, her whole body taut and ready to break apart, and when his thumb pressed against her nub, it was all she could take.

SLOWLY ADAM came alive. First he opened one eye, then the other and stared up at the blue ceiling. Did he have a blue ceiling at his hotel? He pressed the button on his light-up watch and checked the time: 7:21 a.m.

Then the memories came flooding back and he sat upright, a smile on his face. This wasn't a hotel Posturepedic, this was a true, honest-to-God, people-sleep-here-every-night bed.

And right next to him was the lady to whom it belonged.

Jessica lay buried facedown in the pillows, her hair splayed out around her. She didn't stir. Of course, considering the events that had transpired in the shower, on the bathroom floor, the bedroom floor, and finally, in her bed, she had good reason to be tired.

Four good reasons actually. Adam locked his hands behind his head, and leaned back.

They would have to go to work shortly. But not surprisingly at all, he wanted to stay right where he was. So, maybe they'd be a little late. He shrugged, eyeing the bare skin of her back. Maybe a lot late.

Last night he had worked very hard to satisfy her— all within the terms of the bet, of course. It was a tough job, but somebody had to do it, and he liked to think he was the perfect man for the job. Yes, indeedy.

Not that she wasn't pretty capable herself. Oh, no, Miss Jessica Barnes had the most talented mouth he had ever had the pleasure of knowing. There were six days remaining in the bet, but until then, well, a man had to just get creative. For Adam, it had become a challenge. She needed to win. He wanted to give her that, and at the same time, he wanted to show her exactly what she was fast becoming to him.

Inevitable.

Lightly he stroked the curve of her shoulder, and she burrowed obliviously closer to his hand. He smiled.

When he had been involved in relationships before, the image of the perfect woman had become his Holy Grail. She would have a rosebud mouth, just right for those quick goodbye kisses when he left to hit the road. Her hands would be dusted with flour, and he would take off for his next assignment with an image of her ready smile playing in his head.

But here was the perfect woman for him. A wide, full mouth that a man wouldn't ever want to leave, and hands that were quick and efficient. Hands that could bring a man to his knees.

The blankets pooled at her waist and he contented himself with simply stroking her skin. The sun was rising higher in the sky and light was just peeking through the miniblinds, casting her in a golden glow. The bare lines of her back beckoned for more than his touch. Magnificent. He leaned forward, to satisfy himself that this wasn't some dream, but then he tamped down his more selfish urges and, with a great sigh of regret, pulled the blanket up around her shoulders and settled in to guard her sleep.

Two seconds later, she groaned and rolled over, throwing the blanket off.

The selfish urges reared their lurid head, and Adam knew when he was beaten. He raised up on one elbow, leisurely tracing her curves with his eyes, appreciating the round hollow beneath her throat and the perfect lines of her breast.

Her chest rose and fell in a quick rhythm, as if even in sleep, she needed to move. Jessica Barnes would never stay still. No, she needed to reach for something new, bigger and better than before.

Last night that had been him. The sheets tented

around him, tangible proof of exactly how she affected him.

If he didn't do something quickly, he was going to attack her again. *Attack her?* How far the mighty had fallen. Adam had always laughed at the locker-room stories, smugly pleased at his own more refined sensibilities.

Always the man in control. She sighed in her sleep, her mouth curled up in a dreamless smile.

And he was still the man in control. Quickly he climbed out of bed, searched through the dim light for his pants and finally found them buried under two towels and a pair of panty hose.

He grinned and shook his head. Poor girl, too busy working her fingers to the bone to have time to straighten up her room. Well, soon that would change, and she would have more than enough time to relax, read, take long baths, and still keep a great house.

But for now, it was time for breakfast. As he padded into the kitchen, he wondered what she would like. Eggs? Bagels? Cereal? Frowning, he shook off that thought. He'd had enough of hotel breakfast bars to last a lifetime. He opened one door that he thought must pass through to the kitchen, only to discover a utility closet. Shelves of *Money* and *Fortune* magazines were organized neatly, yellow index tabs marking articles of interest. Below that were file boxes, marked Taxes 1994-1998, 1998-2002, 2002-2004.

Obviously this wasn't the kitchen. He padded through the hall back into the living room and called on his navigational instincts. Somewhere in this apartment was a kitchen. He found a coat closet with assorted coats, gloves, hats and umbrellas.

Off the back wall, he found another bedroom, which he assumed she used as her office. No kitchen there.

And just when he was about to give up and ask her, he found the two half-height doors next to the entertainment center. Inside were four bags of chips, a can of salsa, two snack-size packages of cookies, a six-pack of diet soda and a box of Pop-Tarts.

He'd been searching for her kitchen, and instead, he'd found a junk-food wasteland. The job really *was* killing her. He had known she worked long hours and was under so much stress, but he had never dreamed of the extent that it had affected her life. Firmly he closed the doors.

Well, this wasn't going to work. So much for a home-cooked breakfast. Adam finally resigned himself to ordering out—but just for today. He went back into the bedroom, got dressed, and went outside to hunt down breakfast.

THERE WAS a ringing in her head. Insistent, annoying...she threw the pillow over her ears, but still it wouldn't stop.

"What?" she asked, more a rhetorical question than anything else, but she could still hope.

Realizing that the ringing was not responding to her voice, she slowly pulled the pillow away.

It was the phone.

She sat up, instantly realized she had no clothes on and scanned the room for intruders.

And then she remembered. Oh, yeah.

Oh, yeah....

The phone kept on ringing and she picked it up, just as the answering machine kicked in.

"Hello?" she said, clicking the off button on her answering machine, then picking through her pile of laundry until she found something presentable.

Where was Adam?

"Jess, it's Beth. Oh, God, I thought you'd already left for work. Thank goodness you're still there. I need your help."

Jessica pulled on her sweats, noticing the hickey just below her belly button. "Sure, Beth, what do you need?" she answered, feeling very daring and letting her sweat pants hang low so the hickey was framed quite unashamedly.

J Lo, eat your heart out.

She brought her attention from her hickey to the phone, but Beth's response was so quiet that she had to crank up the volume. "What?"

"I need you to stay on the line. There's this man in my store."

Immediately Jessica straightened. "Does he have a gun or is he wearing a trench coat? Beth, you should call the police. What's he doing?"

"He ordered coffee."

Oh, puh-lease. Now Beth was starting to sound like

Mickey. Life was always one big drama. Jessica fell back on the bed. "Beth, you work in a coffee shop. That's to be expected."

"You don't understand. It's his eyes."

She sat up. "Drugs?"

"No, they're just—scary. Empty."

Jessica whispered into the phone. "What's he doing?"

"He sat down. He's drinking his coffee. Wait! Another man just walked in."

"What's he doing?"

"He's coming to the counter," Beth whispered, and then her voice grew louder, "Hold on just a minute, Chief of Police Dealey, I'll get right back to you on that donation..."

Silently Jessica listened as the man ordered a cappuccino. After an eternity, Beth picked up again. "I'm back."

"Beth, I think you're going to be okay."

"Will you talk to me? Better yet, will you come by the store and sit?"

The sound of the front door opening was music to Jessica's ears, as was the rustling of paper bags containing what smelled like fresh blueberry muffins. Her conscience warred with her stomach. "How about I sit and talk to you on the phone? I'm betting they're just two guys drinking coffee." She got up off the bed and walked into the other room, just as Adam was pulling muffins out of the bakery box.

He looked up, saw her on the phone, and smiled.

She mouthed Beth's name and he did a "whatever" shrug. He'd have to meet Beth, too.

"Oh, J, here comes Mrs. Viggorson. I think you're off the hook."

Secretly Jessica watched Adam, not wanting to be caught ogling, but mainly still in shock. It was a good shock, though. He caught her once and looked a little startled himself and Jessica's heart tripped three times. Still, she needed to get back to the phone conversation. "Beth, maybe you shouldn't be working alone. Did you think about finding another job?"

"I think this one's just right for me. I'll be okay, Jess. Thanks for being there."

"S'all right."

"Want to go to that new club in Wicker Park tonight?"

"Wicker Park?" Jessica frowned, eyeing Adam with more hunger than the muffins. "Let me think about it, okay? Have you talked to Cassandra?"

"I should call her, shouldn't I?"

"I think you should, Beth. I bet she'll go. Give me a call if you get stuck again, okay?"

"Roger, J."

After Jessica hung up the phone, the awkward moment came.

"I brought breakfast."

"Good."

"You didn't have much. I couldn't find a kitchen."

"Umm...no."

"But how do you eat?"

"Oh, you know. A little of this. A little of that. Take-out. Processed foods."

He looked pained. "Have a muffin, Jessica."

Out of habit, she flipped on the morning news and they ate while listening to stock market reports and sports coverage. There was a discrete distance between them, and it might as well have been the Grand Canyon.

What should she say? The silence grew longer, beyond pleasant companionship, and into the silence of two people trying to reconcile fabulous sex with reality.

Intently she watched the screen. He should have said something. He was the consultant. He talked for a living. Oh, God, he wanted to leave.

To salvage her pride, Jessica walked into the bedroom. "I've got a meeting at ten," she said, lying through her teeth, but wanting to have him walk away from her leaving her pride intact.

Time to get dressed and go to work and live her life. In the bowels of her closet, she found her nicest suit.

"Jessica," he said from somewhere really close by.

She turned and he was standing in the doorway.

She smiled up at him, a fake "I'll be okay if you need to leave" smile.

Adam took two steps closer, his face not wearing an apologetic "I need to leave" smile. That was good. He looked intent, serious, and she didn't know if that fell in the bad or good category.

"I have to go into the office..." he started, and she realized that this *was* the "I need to leave" speech.

She stood and held up her dress so that he couldn't see her hickey. That would be for her eyes alone now. "I understand."

He sat down. "That came out wrong. Sorry. Rewind. I do need to leave soon, but I wanted to tell you how much fun I had last night. All of it. Practice, and then...later."

Oh. This was good. She sank into the carpet, her dress falling beside her. "I did, too."

"We didn't talk much..."

She began to smile. "No."

"And I know work is eating you up right now, but everything's going to be all right. I swear I'll make things right for you."

When he looked at her like that, she believed him. "By all rights, I should really hate you," she began.

He flinched, but his gaze returned to hers. "I want us to be together. I don't know how all this is going to play out, but I know that, Jessica."

"I'm afraid about losing more than the bet, Adam."

"You don't have to be afraid."

"Why?" she asked, more bravely than she felt.

"I've got some ideas," he said, a vague answer if ever there was one.

Thoughtfully she studied him, considering whether to press him for more, or whether this was the time to wait. He looked sincere, his gaze soft and steady, and she had her answer. She trusted him. Probably stupid, but there it was.

"Six days left, you know. You're going to lose, Taylor."

The quick grin returned and for the moment the tension was gone. "I've got an idea. We've got six days before this damnable bet is over. Since, uh, foreplay is allowed, how about something a little new? I'll make you come, say, twenty-four times before the end. *All* foreplay."

Just the thought had her thighs throbbing with delight. "Four times a day for the next six days? I know there's a catch somewhere."

"I know. You can cook for me sometime." He looked around her bedroom. "My kitchen."

Cooking? That was a piece of cake. "Sounds like I'm getting the better end of the deal." She eyed his lean hips, his pants tenting in just the right places.

"I'm an unselfish man," he said.

"I think I'm in love."

He dived for her and pulled her on top of him for a heart-stopping kiss. To hell with work. If she was going to be unemployed, she might as well go out with a bang. He rolled them both over until he was pressing her into the carpet, and then his lips began.

"Number one..."

JESSICA FINALLY DRAGGED herself into work at noon. No one seemed to notice that she'd been missing most of the morning, or that Adam had been missing, as well.

He came by her office twice. First to borrow a paper clip, and the second time because he wanted to take her out to dinner.

She smiled and accepted because she knew he owed her two more orgasms before midnight. It was a hard-knocks life, indeed.

He drove her home that night, and they made their way through the parking garage, stealing kisses behind every post. Her parking garage had seventeen posts. She hadn't noticed that before. In the elevator he was gunning for Big O number three on the day, but there were only a few floors to go.

She smiled when the elevator dinged. "Better luck next time, buddy. You're not off the hook yet."

They got to her front door and he jumped her before she got the key in her lock. For a few helpless moments she succumbed to his drugging kiss, but finally she remembered that it was a public hallway.

She shook her head, and pulled him inside.

When the door clicked shut, she nodded her head. "Now."

His eyes gleamed and he sat her down on the couch, seating himself beside her. "First of all, we start with the neck." He pressed a lingering kiss under her ear. "You taste delicious."

As he trailed his lips down lower, she sank farther into the cushions.

"Next we explore the collarbone, right here," he whispered, nipping at the soft flesh at the base of her throat. Not having the strength to resist, Jessica leaned her head back against the soft material of her couch.

Gently his hands worked the buttons on her blouse, pushing aside the material inch by inch. "Next, we need to get you comfortable, sweetheart."

A touch here, a soft stroke there. Each caress made her breath come faster.

Soon her blouse and bra were disposed of, and he looked into her eyes with such heat and desire. Her nipples hardened in anticipation and he didn't disappoint her. His hands were large, his fingers rough, and as he stroked her breasts, she shivered with warmth.

It wasn't enough. He pressed her down against the cushions and began to stroke her thighs, pushing her skirt higher with each stroke. Teasing, wicked. She moaned and curled her hips upward. But he would not be dissuaded. A lock of hair fell into his eyes, such an odd sight. His hair was usually perfectly ordered, but she focused on the few strands, holding tight to her sanity.

"I want to touch you, Jessica. Is that all right?" he asked, a stupidly rhetorical question that was only designed to drive her closer to the edge.

She nodded quickly.

His fingers flirted with the edge of her panties, slowly tracing a line in the sensitive crevice where her thigh ended. "Such marvelous skin." He moved the edge of nylon back and pressed a soft kiss where his fingers had been.

Then his fingers returned and cupped her sex through the sheer material. "So wet."

She raised her hips to meet his hand more fully and his hand began to knead her. Helplessly her legs slid open, and he pressed more firmly. Faster and faster he stroked, his eyes focused on her face, smiling when her hips rose higher against him. When she couldn't take anymore, his finger slid inside her, slipping between her lips and playing her as sweetly as a song.

She closed her eyes, unable to bear the brightness of the light, and her hips moved against him, searching for relief.

"That's it, Jess. That's it."

He whispered the words, over and over, and she followed his spell. Closer and closer she moved to the edge. Eventually, she could stand no more. Her muscles tightened, and her heart stopped. One, two, three. And then she was alive once more.

When she opened her eyes again, he was watching her. She expected a joke, a smug look of victory. The humor seemed to keep a barrier between them, but there was such tenderness in his eyes this time. Somehow the world had narrowed down to this one moment. No jobs, no bets, no time for competitions.

He stayed with her through the night. They didn't say much. Something had changed and neither chose to question it, as if words would unseat the shaky foundation that was slowly being built beneath them.

Each night that week he stayed with her, going to his hotel after work and bringing a fresh change of clothes. He helped her with track practice, made a few calls to caterers, and in general, made each day heaven. And at night? He didn't make love to her fully, but that didn't keep him from finding new ways to pleasure her. Some nights were silly, some nights were sweet, but each night before they fell asleep exhausted, he would press a kiss to her lips. Jessica stopped considering the future. The present was too dazzling to see beyond.

THERE WAS no place in Chicago like the Wrigley Field bleachers on a Sunday afternoon early in May. Today the breeze had kicked up to high, but it was blowing across the lake, so the pitchers would have a field day. For the fans, it meant gloves out, balls flying through the air. For Jessica, it meant home-run heaven.

Adam had taken the gentlemanly trek to procure two beverages of choice, which, without question for a Cubs game, was beer. While he was gone, Jessica scanned the stands, on the lookout for Mickey and Adam's friend—Pete O'Connell. She also scanned the bleachers for any two-bit fans of the Cardinals that had happened to con their way into the sacred territory.

"Yo, Crudale, 1975 called and they want your haircut back," came from two rows behind her, and she turned to give a big thumbs-up to the heckler, a blonde outfitted in a tank top, who was clearly on the make. Jessica remembered those days and sighed with contentment. There was a lot to be said for being in a relationship.

When she turned back around, Adam was just heading up into the stands and she watched him with approval, noticing the appraising glances from the fans of the feminine persuasion.

Yeah, that was hers. The Cubbies jersey looked oh, so appealing, and she was glad she'd bought it for him. Her first present to him, which was a big step.

"Hit it with your purse, you bum," came another shout from way up high and Adam turned to look up, a little startled.

Jessica smiled. He really did need to learn to relax.

Two seconds later, he sank down into the seat next to her and handed her the beer and peanuts. "One Old Style, coming up."

Jessica took a long sip and sighed. Just because he was so nice, she gave him a kiss, too.

"What was that for?" he asked.

"What can I say? Baseball makes me happy." She leaned back, letting the sun warm her cheeks. "It's great, isn't it?"

"Yeah," he said with his practiced consultant's nod, which she was fast learning to recognize. He truly was one of the unbelievers.

"Wait until the game starts."

"Can't wait," he said, still looking a little nervous.

The star pitcher from the Cardinals trotted on to the field and waved to the fans. Next to Jessica, two teenage boys stood and booed. Jessica twitched in her seat, but Adam seemed completely oblivious to all the excitement in the air, and she didn't really think he'd take it too well if he knew just how foul her mouth could get—but only during sports.

"Great day for catching some rays?"

"Yeah."

"So, have you been to a game before?"

"A professional game, a Cubs game or a baseball game?"

"Any."

Adam shrugged. "None."

What a sheltered life he had led. She couldn't imagine life without professional sports. "No kidding! Drink your beer, farm boy. We've got some educating to do." She pointed ahead. "Okay, this is a baseball diamond."

He rolled his eyes. "I know how the game is played."

"Well, you know, Alabama is defined as a rural community."

"You're going to pay for that remark, Barnes."

Jessica wiggled her eyebrows. "I live for retribution."

His gaze dropped down to her mouth, so intent that she found herself licking suddenly dry lips.

When he looked back up, the fire had dimmed. "You love baseball, I take it."

"And football, and hockey and basketball. The Bears, 1986 World Champions. Da Bulls, World

Champions, '91, '92, '93..." she took a breath "...'96, '97, '98. Let us not forget hockey. Blackhawks, World Champions, '34, '38, and '61. White Sox, World Champions, 1906, 1917..." she took another breath "...and last, but certainly never least, Chicago Cubs, World Champions, 1907 and 1908. Hell, it's Chicago." Whoops. A mild slip-up in language vulgarity. She hoped he didn't notice.

He didn't—no, no, no. Instead, being the cutthroat competitor that he was, he pounced immediately on the weakest link. "Champions in 1908, huh? Here it is, what, ninety-six years later?"

Jessica didn't budge. "Cubs fans will always believe."

"We'll see what you say after the next fifty years of losses."

She shot him a superior look. "Yes, we will." And then she changed the subject. "Look, there's Mickey and—is that Pete?"

Adam just laughed. "Yeah, the one in the tie. That's Pete."

"Oh, my. Mickey's going to tear him up and spit him out."

They watched as Mickey led the way, pretty much ignoring Pete, which Jessica couldn't blame her for. A tie? Adam just grimaced. "I hope that's only an expression."

"You never know with Mick." Jessica stood and waved. "Mickey! Over here!"

Mickey and Pete walked over to section 146 and

crawled through the bleachers, dislodging popcorn and one mildly drunk frat boy in the process.

"Good afternoon, all. Jess, you brought your glove?"

"He he he... Does the sun rise in the east?" Jessica pulled her glove out from under the seat.

Mickey popped out of her seat. "Hey, Foster, you're nothing but a bench polisher. Go sit down and let a real man play."

Wanting nothing more than to stand up and give them hell—heck—as well, Jessica took a quick glance at Adam's impassive face and sat on her hands. Quickly she checked her watch. Fifteen minutes to game time. Surely she could last out nine innings.

Needing a diversion from the melee on the field, she turned to Pete. "You must be Pete."

Adam quickly jumped in, polite-host style. "God, I'm such a slacker. Pete, this is Jessica Barnes. Jessica, this is Pete O'Connell."

Pete sat forward, looking around Mickey, which earned him no points. "Adam tells me that you're a star over at Hard-Wire. What a story. I've been following it in the paper."

Adam coughed. "Yeah, that's been real nice, but you know, Jessica's the kind of person that could be whatever she wanted."

"Well, maybe," Jessica said.

Mickey sat back down and began shelling peanuts—onto Pete's polished wing-tip shoes. He was either too ignorant or too polite to make a scene. Mickey then smiled at the mess she was making. Was it any wonder the woman had troubles with men? She looked up, devious as ever. "Nah, J is going to be the first vice president in the Barnes family. Unless she gets beat out by her little brother, that is."

Jessica shot Mickey an evil glare. "There is no way—" and then she noticed Adam's interested expression "—that the Cubbies are going to lose today. No sirree. It's a great day for ball!"

Behind her prescription sunglasses, Mickey just smiled.

The first inning was uneventful. Two hits by the Cardinals, but the inning ended with both batters still on base. The Cubbies were three up, three down.

Adam talked Medicare reform with Pete. Mickey made faces behind Pete's back.

In the second inning, Davis hit a homer directly toward left field. Jessica stood and watched it fly right into some tourist's hand. "Damn!"

"Hand me that thing," Adam said, pointing to her glove.

"You're going to catch a ball?"

"Is that what you want?"

"Of course."

"Then that's what I'm going to do."

Mickey followed the whole interchange and flashed a thumbs-up of approval behind Adam's back. Jessica shrugged in a "Yeah, I know, but don't want to brag" sort of way.

By the fourth inning, Jessica and Mickey were sitting together, Pete was playing flirty-eyes with the stacked blonde two rows back and Adam was pounding the glove like a professional. There was hope for him yet.

The Cardinals were up, and Foster pounded a ball up, up, up, right...over...Jessica's...head.

The glove shot up and the ball landed home. Adam took the ball and handed it to Jessica. "It's not every man who gives a lady his balls. I hope you appreciate it."

The stacked blonde led the crowd into the appropriate cheer before Jessica had time to rescue Adam. *"Throw it back!"*

Adam looked confused.

For the first time since she'd known him, Jessica felt a twinge of sympathy. She stood, gave him a lingering glance, and threw the ball back onto the field.

"What did you do that for?"

Mindful of the glares from all directions, Jessica motioned Adam to sit down. Mickey, being no help at all, was merely cracking up. Jessica pitched her voice down low, hoping to hide the fact that her boyfriend was a Cubs neophyte. "You can't keep it."

"Why not?" Adam whispered back.

"If the Cubs don't hit it, it's, well, kinda tainted."

"So, not only do I have to catch another home run, now you're telling me it has to be a Cubs home run?"

Jessica nodded quickly. "But you can do it. I believe in you."

Adam met her eyes for a long moment, his look considering. "You're *really* going to owe me for this, Barnes."

She leaned over, kissed him one more time. For luck, for being clueless and chivalrous all at the same time, and most of all, for being Adam. "Just remember. Foreplay is allowed."

And that shut him up very nicely.

10

BY THE seventh-inning stretch, Jessica had forgotten all about her good intentions. When the umpire blew the call at second, Jessica rained curses on his mother, his wife and his dog.

By the eighth inning, Adam had learned several colorful Chicago phrases and knew exactly when to stand and when not to. Proudly he caught Davis's second homer and gave it to Jessica.

In the ninth inning, a freckle-faced teenager popped up behind them and caught Davis's third homer of the day. Adam noticed Mickey's distress and, like any good errant knight, sprang into action.

Jessica watched in awe as he complimented the boy on his exquisite catching talents, used a melancholy foot-shuffle to accentuate his plight, and then gave the boy not one, but two, Ulysses S. Grant portraits to use for a future scholarship fund. Jessica rolled her eyes at that one, but when he presented the ball to Mickey, Jessica's fate was sealed.

Without a doubt, she was in love.

IT WAS after dark when they got back to Jessica's apartment. It was the last day of the bet, and only a few more hours remained. The days of four hours of foreplay were going to be gone like water under the bridge, but the idea of Adam Taylor and full penetration made her knees go weak.

And of course, since there were five more hours to go, she found herself spoiling for a fight. Anything to release some pent-up energy.

"The date was a complete bust, you know," she said.

Adam tossed his keys on the coffee table. "It's going to be tough finding a guy for Mickey. Has she tried the Internet?" he asked, settling on the couch.

Jessica stretched out next to him, her head in his lap, feeling his pent-up energy as well. Masterfully she ignored it. "Oh, come on, Pete is a brownnosing dweeb. He took every chance he could get to suck up to you. Maybe he's gay?"

"No, he's not gay. He wouldn't have taken home the blonde if he wasn't a fully functioning, red-blooded, American male."

"You say that like you noticed her."

Adam looked at her in surprise. "You're jealous, aren't you?"

"Are you kidding? Of her? Of course, I'm not jealous. I may not have surgically enhanced bazoombas, but I feel adequately endowed."

"Adequate? Oh, babe. I can think of ten thousand adjectives to describe your bazoombas, and none of them remotely resemble *adequate*."

Jessica raised up and stared at him down her nose. "Like what?"

"Cute."

She glared and then peeked down her shirt just to make sure he was kidding. "Nope."

"Pert."

"That's a shampoo."

"You're joking?"

"Nope, try again."

"Taut."

"Better." She unbuttoned the top two buttons on her jersey.

Adam looked on in interest. "Rosy."

"Oh, now you're getting the hang of it." Jessica unbuttoned the last of the jersey, letting it hang temptingly open. Today she had opted to go braless—a freedom enjoyed by those of the less-than-endowed club—and her cleavage, while not enough to write home about, still left a mysterious shadow.

"Liberated?"

She leaned toward him, the shirt gaping nicely. "Keep going."

His jaw tightened immeasurably. "What time is it?"

"Seven o'clock," she said, still waiting for what came after *liberated*.

"Five more hours. God help me, I've never been so happy to see midnight before."

"Look, I understand that you're feeling some pressure downstairs about now, but my breasts are still anticipating what comes next."

Then he broke into a grin and ripped off her shirt in a gesture that was going to make it into the diary. "You know, I really love it when you get feisty."

He pushed her back into the pillows and gave her breasts the attention they craved. After a few more diary-worthy moments, he looked up and grinned. "Ripe. Definitely ripe."

WHILE ADAM showered, Jessica took special precautions to make sure that when the clock chimed midnight everything was absolutely perfect. A bottle of wine sat chilling in a bucket of ice, she misted the air with her favorite perfume. The lights were all off except for the bedside lamp that shone with a muted glow. Her trusty 200-count cotton sheets had been replaced with white satin ones, and from a box hidden in the back corner of her closet, she pulled out the secret box that contained a wispy piece of lingerie that was guaranteed to drive a man wild.

Adam walked into the bedroom, his hair still damp and tousled, wearing a right-wing-conservative set of white boxers that by all rights should not appear so sexy. On him, they were almost illegal. She pulled her terry cloth robe tighter and hid the box behind her.

For the first time, he noticed the extra accoutrements in the room and gave her a long, appraising glance. Jessica merely smiled in her best smoky manner just to give him something more to think about.

"I'll be back in a minute," she said as she walked out of the room to change clothes.

The merry widow took some time to get just right, and she pulled and hooked and studied and adjusted.

"You all right in there?" he asked.

"Be out soon," she yelled back, pulling the peek-a-boo bodice down just a little bit lower.

Finally, everything was perfect.

When she walked into the room, he was sitting on the bed waiting patiently, and she stood framed in the doorway, hoping and praying that her efforts would be suitably appreciated.

And when his gaze roved over her—twice—she knew they were.

He was speechless when she walked over to him, and because she was just a little bit nervous, her voice shook as she asked, "See something you like?"

Bemusedly he shook his head and held out a hand to her. "I'm just trying to breathe here."

"Please don't die on me. Not yet."

He pulled her closer, so her legs straddled his thigh, the hard pulse inside her starting all over again. "Trust me, my plans for the next few hours have nothing to do with dying."

"Good," was about all she could manage.

His hands cupped her bottom, his eyes closing for just a moment as his fingers caressed her bare flesh. "So, Barnes, how does it feel to win?"

She rocked against his thigh, the hard muscles on his leg pushing against her sex. She closed her eyes, blocking out the hunger in his. She couldn't think when he looked at her like that. "It's weird. Com-

pletely abnormal. This week I've been so busy anticipating right now, I haven't worried about it."

Then he laughed, husky, low, and she opened her
eyes. Mindlessly, she rubbed her sex against his leg,
sending moisture pooling between her thighs.

He met her eyes, and she shivered with the intensity
there. There was the hunger she had seen, a hunger
echoed inside herself. And possession. A primal look
that made her sensually aware of the differences between them.

He pulled at the black straps, letting them hang
down low until her nipples were just peeking over the
top. The ruffled edge grazed against her soft flesh
when she moved, and her breasts swelled against the
pressure. She ran her hands up over his shoulders,
loving the feel of the solid flesh beneath her fingers.

"I wanted to take it slow tonight, Barnes, but you're
making it awfully difficult."

She smiled at him, a slow smile that told him all he
was asking.

His mouth covered hers and French-kissed her until
their bodies were rocking in time to his brazen tongue.
Then he slid her forward, her thighs cupping his
prominent erection and something akin to a purr escaped from her. There was a time for slow and now
wasn't it.

He stood and stripped off his shorts and—Holy Mo-
ley. Jessica only hoped that she wasn't gaping. But he
didn't notice. Instead, he sheathed himself in a con-

dom and brought her down on top of him with one powerful thrust.

Instantly she moved against him, her body taking over, its response preordained.

His hands gripped her hips and lifted her, causing the magical sensation to leave. Impatiently she sank down on him, seeking his flesh once more. Again he lifted her and the pattern continued. Each time she felt her muscles grow tighter and tighter.

Mindlessly she moved, her senses sharp and sensitive. Neither spoke, only the slap of flesh and the heavy sounds of their breathing broke the silence.

And eventually the sounds faded, leaving only the bright fullness of her pleasure, so intense it was almost painful. She collapsed against him, his skin warm and damp. He found her lips, kissed her until the trembling inside her started all over again, and with their bodies still joined, rolled her back onto the bed.

And started all over again.

IT WAS a long time later; she lay curled against him on the bed. Slowly he stroked her hair, tangling his fingers in the silky strands. His body had found its release, and now his heart needed a release of its own.

"I love you, Jessica." He spoke quietly, speaking words he'd never said before.

She lay still, so still that he tensed, wondering if he had misread her. Wondering if something that made him feel so alive could have been manufactured in his own mind.

She didn't say anything, merely turned in his arms and looked at him, and there were two tears running down her cheeks.

He had wanted to hear her answer him back. Wanted her to confess that she loved him madly. Not that he deserved it, but still, he wanted to believe, he wanted to hope.

Translation: He wanted to live.

Gently he kissed the tears away and, with a heavy heart, he made love to her once more.

THE NIGHT passed quickly from carnal bliss into a relentless insecurity. That's what happened when you spent eleven years working to overcome the infamous loser label. Next to her, Adam was awake as well, so she gathered her courage. Finally it was time for the gazillion-dollar question.

"Adam, what's going to happen to me?"

He rubbed a hand over his eyes, not misunderstanding at all. "The deal's not completely done, Jessica."

"No, but it's looking good, isn't it?"

"Yeah."

The short, noncommittal answers always worried her the most. "Finance is going to get cut."

"Most likely. It's redundant."

"Gee, thanks."

He rolled up on one elbow and shook his head. "Jessica, a job isn't worth the pain."

There was a time for clichés and now wasn't it. She smiled tightly. "I feel so much better. Thank you."

And Adam, who must have more patience than anyone else she ever knew, didn't get mad. Rather he pushed the hair away from her eyes and sweetly stroked her face. "What do you want to do? You could come home with me. I'll have a place for you, Jessica. I'll always have a place for you."

"I liked my life. Really did. Now I'm just a little scared. Can I think about it?"

His smile faded. Such absolute uncertainty probably wasn't good for a man's ego, but Jessica had issues of her own.

Then he kissed her, his body covering hers, and Jessica was quickly overcome by the magic, drugging feeling that he inspired in her. When he kissed her, when he held her in his arms, she felt as if she could do anything.

He made love to her once more, and suddenly Alabama didn't look so bad to her.

THE NEXT TWO WEEKS passed quickly. Jessica had practice with the girls' team on Monday and they moved to twice a week as the meet drew closer. They had elected to be called the Flames, and Jessica had jerseys printed up with the new logo on it. With each practice, the girls got faster and more focused. She was betting that there was nobody that could beat them now.

She spent Tuesdays after work at Beth's coffee shop. Adam was working late. A presentation was due at the end of the month, and lately work had been eerily quiet.

The week before her Mom's party, she arranged for the last-minute preparations. It was going be a smashing success. The flowers would be delivered early Saturday. She'd paid a deposit to a string quartet from Milwaukee who'd gotten a great review in the *Sun-Times,* and the RSVP calls had begun flooding in.

And then there was Adam.

Everything should have been great. After all, he loved her. He was wonderful and attentive, always there with a smile and a kiss. No one at work knew of their relationship and they chose to keep it that way. He spent more nights than not with her, and at night, when she fell asleep in his arms, she'd listen as he talked about his house back in Alabama and his big plans for it. A few more times he mentioned her coming with him to see it, which, as she knew, meant after his Hard-Wire contract was complete and he had left Chicago. All of which Jessica never brought up again; she was a firm believer in the "If you don't talk about, it'll never happen" rule.

He had been trying to teach her how to cook, which was more difficult than it seemed because she basically had no kitchen and she was doing okay. She'd bought a minifridge and a George Foreman grill, and had now perfected the hamburger.

One time she'd actually cooked in his hotel suite. As a career in the culinary arts, it made for a slow start.

Yup, everything should have been great, instead it

felt oddly surreal. As if someone else was living her life and had turned it into a fairy tale.

Each day she went to work, proving to herself that yes, this was Jessica Barnes's life, but even at work there were changes. Small and subtle, but she could read the signs.

By the first Thursday morning in June, at approximately ten o'clock, Jessica had tangible evidence that something was up. She'd only received three e-mails, and two were from her brother, Ian. There was no urgent "I need this number" from Artie, or a "Can you find out how much we spent on coffee last month?" from Garrison.

Adam had left for O'Hare at 4:30 a.m.—a flight to San Jose, which they didn't really discuss, but she knew which company was headquartered in San Jose. It would take a particularly lovesick lemming not to notice the telltale empty in-box.

This wasn't a problem that Adam could solve. This wasn't a problem that would go away with a smile and a kiss. There weren't many places Jessica could turn to with this one, so she turned to her computer.

Jessica says: "Mickey?"

Mickey says: "Yes?"

Jessica says: "What are you doing?"

Mickey says: "You're bored, aren't you? Where's lover boy?"

Jessica says: "Don't be snippy."

Mickey says: "Oh, no, you probably spent all weekend with your date. I, on the other hand, got passed over by a peroxide blonde and I'm being *snippy*."

Jessica says (feeling as if she'd been so mired in her own problems that she'd completely overlooked Mickey's, but knowing that her own misery made true consolation impossible): "You're still sore about that? He was a dweeb."

Mickey says: "If you're trying to make me feel better, you're failing. Now I've been passed over by a dweeb."

Jessica says: "He didn't deserve you."

Mickey says: "Yeah, I know. But I *really want to have sex*."

Jessica says (in the face of Mickey's misery, actually starting to feel better): "Have you tried putting that on a business card? I bet it would work."

Mickey says: "I'm not desperate."

Jessica says: "Yes, you are."

Mickey says (while eyeing studmo intern with a lustful gleam): "You're only saying that because you're the one getting laid."

Jessica says (smugly): "Possibly, but I'm not spilling details."

Mickey says: "Yeah, bully for you. Forgive me if I sound insanely jealous. It's because I *am*."

Jessica says (wanting to change subject from Mickey-angst to Jessica-angst because, although Mickey did not currently have a love life or potential for love life, Mickey looked to be gainfully employed until her Social Security kicked in): "Can you send me an e-mail? Just to see if it gets through? Maybe we're having network problems."

Mickey says: "Done."

Jessica says (with a heavy sigh): "I got it."

Mickey says: "Why do you think you're having problems?"

Jessica says: "I haven't gotten any e-mails today. Well, except for some dirty jokes from Ian, but I mean stuff from important people."

Mickey says (while shaking her head sadly and managing virtual sympathy hugs for her friend): "Got your résumé polished?"

Jessica says: "That's what I was thinking, too. Secretly I kept thinking that everything would turn out OK."

Mickey says: "Why don't you ask him?"

Jessica says (biting her nails): "He's told me not to worry."

Mickey says: "That's easy for him to say. He's the man wielding the ax."

Jessica says (thinking a long time before actually writing out the words): "He wants me to go back to Alabama with him."

Mickey says: "*What?*"

Jessica says: "I mean, he hasn't come right out and like, proposed or anything, but he talks about his house, and he talks about how lonely his job is, and he talks about how he wants to have someone to come home to."

Mickey says: "Tell him to buy a dog."

Jessica says (still thinking very hard): "It wouldn't be so bad."

Mickey says: "Oh, he must be really, really good."

Jessica says: "I shouldn't say anything. I certainly won't deny it."

Mickey says: "What would you do in Alabama?"

Jessica says (in a whisper): "Make cookies, vacuum, birth babies."

Mickey says: "Oh, how the mighty have fallen."

Jessica says (clapping hands over her ears): "Shutupshutupshutupshutup."

Mickey says: "Is this what's going to make you happy? I mean, how long have you known the guy? Have you even *been* to Alabama?"

Jessica says: "I drove through it once on the way to Fort Lauderdale."

Mickey says: "Oh, yeah. I forgot about that trip. Remember the cheese puffs?"

Jessica says (not really wanting to talk about the cheese puffs): "He's the one, Mick. And maybe I'm missing out on being a well-rounded woman by not exploring the domestic arts."

Mickey says: "You mean the dark arts."

Jessica says (while sneezing): "My mom did it."

Mickey says: "And you've sworn since you were in fourth grade that you never would."

Jessica says: "I can change my mind."

Mickey says: "Okay, I can understand about the kids thing. They're cute. I can even understand the cookie thing, although I don't think I want to be there when he learns you can't boil water. But vacuuming? Who in their right mind gets titillated by a Hoover?"

Jessica says: "Okay, it's not on my top ten list of turn-ons, you know? But..."

Mickey says: "But, schmut. You're being a wimp, J."

Jessica says: "I'm in love."

Mickey says (sensing the truth when it smacks her over the head): "Okay, we can do the bachelorette combo going-away party, but I want a stripper."

Jessica says: "I'd miss you, Mick."

Mickey says (with one tiny noise that might have been a sniff): "Don't get mushy."

Jessica says: "I could have a computer with a DSL line put in at the house. We could IM each other, just like old times."

Mickey says (without enthusiasm and thinking that Alabama is a long-ass way away): "Sounds like a smegging good time."

Jessica says: "Promise me you'll be at Mom's party next week."

Mickey says: "Is Adam bringing any friends?"

Jessica says: "No."

Mickey says: "Okay. I'll be there."

THE PLANE RIDE back to Chicago was just about the longest, bumpiest, most annoying flight he'd ever been on.

Translation: The deal was done.

Adam sat in first class, the one perk he earned by

being a Super-Duper Gold-Platinum-Diamond frequent flier, and allowed himself to get quietly drunk.

Number 44713 was getting cut. In the back of his
mind, he'd held out hopes that something would
change, but after today, it was a done deal. He'd sat
there in the meeting, at Phil Osterson's right hand,
beaming his best "I'm your man" smile to JCN as he
delivered the report. They'd been pleased, wearing
their "We just bought twenty percent market share"
smiles. And after the papers were signed, they'd taken
him out to dinner. JCN had picked up the tab. The
price? Thirty pieces of silver.

Everything had always been easy for him before.
Now there wasn't a day that went by that he didn't
dread logging on to his computer. It was like a video
game, but those weren't cartoon characters anymore,
those were real people whose heads he was whacking
off.

At least he had something he could offer Jessica in
return.

The attendant came by and asked him if he wanted
another drink. Adam, possibly because he had a little
sense left, declined. With two hours left on the flight,
he needed to sober up.

After all, it was tonight he intended to propose.

11

BY MIDNIGHT, Jessica had abandoned all hope that Adam would show up and had donned her favorite T-shirt and crawled into bed. Alone.

After tossing and turning, she turned on the TV and watched four episodes of "Hometime." How to waterproof your basement. Of course, she didn't think they had basements in Alabama. Replacing a shower stall, which she downloaded the notes for from her laptop. That one would come in handy. The third episode was building a playscape. It seemed a little early, but she was twenty-nine, so she downloaded the notes for that show as well. The last episode was installing a home office, which shouldn't have made her cry, but did.

At one-thirty the doorbell rang, and she had never been more grateful for the diversion. She needed him to hold her, to remind her exactly why Alabama would be her own paradise.

When she opened the door, he didn't speak, just locked the door and took her on the coffee table there in the dark. She held on to his shoulders, letting him pound inside her. At first she wondered what was wrong. This wasn't like Adam, not at all, but then thought became more difficult and she simply held to his shoulders for support, her pleasure washing away all of the worries that she'd been carrying.

It was some time later when she emerged from the fog, and they were sprawled on the carpet, clothing askew.

"Welcome home," she said, waiting for the room to quit spinning.

"I should apologize."

Jessica smiled, a little tired, a little sore, but mostly happy. "Never apologize for great sex."

"Was that great sex?" he asked, his voice raspy.

"Always, Adam. Always," she said, reaching out for his hand in the darkness.

"I love you, Jessica."

Her heart stopped. He'd only said it the one other time, and she couldn't get used to it. "Just because of the great sex?" she asked with a fake laugh.

He turned to her, and more than anything she wished it wasn't dark, wished she could see his eyes, judge for herself what was going on. "No. I love you because you're Jessica. I never knew a Jessica before and I'm glad I never did, because you're the only one of you in my heart. I always figured I wanted somebody to come home to, but hell, I never imagined it'd be somebody I never wanted to leave."

Jessica realized that ignoring the problem wouldn't make it go away, so she took a deep breath and put it out on the table. "We'd live in Alabama?"

"I know it's asking a lot of you, but come back with

me. We'll fly out next weekend. You can see the house. I know you'll love it. Valley Head is a great little town. It's just down from where I grew up. We can hit some antique stores, or whatever kind of stores you want. It'll be your house, Jessica. Our home."

For a long, long time she could close her eyes and imagine ivy-covered chimneys and tall windows that would sparkle in the sun. Big yellow roses that climbed on a white trellis. A big rambling house that would be filled with love. Shouldn't that be enough? Jessica felt a sneeze coming on, but she managed to avoid it. "No job, huh?"

He pulled her into the crook of his arm and she rested her head on his chest. His heart pumped so reliably and she listened to the steady rhythm. "I'm sorry," was all he said.

"What's the main industry around your place?" she asked, still hopeful.

"Agriculture, and there are four bed-and-breakfasts, and one Waffle House."

So this was to be her reality. A fairy-tale life complete with handsome prince and ivy-covered castle walls. Well, what's good enough for Cinderella was good enough for her.

"Jess, you don't want to be stuck in corporate politics for the rest of your life." He laughed, not in a funny way. "You're above all that. All the lies and backstabbing. Is that really what you want?"

She wanted to say yes, but then what sort of idiot would she be? "You know what I want? I want to be with you. I want to be there when you come home. I want to have kids with you. Bratty, runny-nose, never-sleep-at-night hellions that look just like us. I'm not sure about the cooking and cleaning stuff—"

Adam didn't even hesitate. "We can hire help."

"Well, there you go. Problem solved. How can I say no?"

"I got a ring for you—it's in my briefcase."

A ring. He'd bought her a ring. Oh God, she was going to cry again. "Can I see?"

He laughed and sat up. "This wasn't exactly how I intended to propose, but..." His voice trailed up and he opened his case. "I hope you like it. I probably should have taken you with me, but I had hoped I could surprise you."

She flipped on the lights and he handed her a small velvet box. When she opened the lid, tears pricked at the corners of her eyes. It was the Perfect Ring. A small square-cut diamond, with two chips on either side, all neatly set in an old-fashioned platinum band.

Then he put the ring on her finger. Like magic, it fit perfectly.

Now Jessica was crying for real. "I love you, Adam. And not because you have great taste in rings."

He pulled her close and stroked her hair. "We'll figure something out, Jess. If you want to work, or paint, or even start your own business, it'd be okay with me."

She looked up, and now she could see what she had needed to see before. There was love in his eyes. And for now, that was enough. She knew she wanted to take care of him and everything else.

Blissfully, she shrugged it off. "I think I'll worry about that tomorrow."

TELLING HER FRIENDS she was getting married was going to be difficult. Jessica wrestled with the different options for disclosure and finally settled on the familiar. So at 11:00 a.m. Saturday morning, she had them all meet her at the bar.

She bought four martinis and lined them up along the polished wooden surface that had witnessed more than a few moments of abject stupidity. Quickly she downed one martini, and then replaced it before the others arrived. Alcohol was a wonderful confidence booster and her confidence currently needed some boosting.

Cassandra was the first to arrive. Impeccably dressed as always in a scandalous red skirt and shoes that defied gravity.

At the four glasses, she raised one brow. "Eleven in the morning. Martinis? It's either something marvelous or else someone died."

But wisely Cassandra didn't ask. Instead she sat down, and then just like old times, they scoped out the bar, laughing and comparing opinions.

Beth and Mickey came together and Beth instantly noticed the ring. Then there were hugs, one or two toasts, and the third degree began.

"How did he propose?"

Jessica edited that part.

"When's the big day?"

"Don't know. Haven't got that far in the plans."

"What do your parents think?"

"Don't know, haven't told them yet."

"Will y'all find a house in the city, or are you going to drive a minivan in the burbs?"

Jessica worked to make a smile. "We're going to move," she answered, not meeting Mickey's eyes.

"No," said Beth in a shocked voice. Clearly this was not an option she had considered.

"Where to?" asked Cassandra in that cool tone of hers. Cassandra was never surprised about anything.

Jessica took a long sip of the martini. "Alabama," she answered.

Mickey stayed quiet. No one really noticed except for Jessica, who knew exactly what she was thinking. That was the bummer thing about best-friend sensory perception. It worked with the bad as well as the good.

"So, you're going to work down there?" Beth asked, always helpful.

"It's sorta isolated. Lots of farming, big mountains, well, as big as they get in Alabama. Really nice," Jessica replied automatically.

Eventually, Beth dragged Cassandra off to go buy bridal magazines and left Jessica alone to deal with issues. She sighed.

"Congratulations," said Mick, drinking her martini with more gusto than usual.

Jessica signaled the cute bartender for another round. "Thanks."

They sat there, sipping drinks, the silence deafening.

Finally, unable to stand it, Jessica jumped in, feet-first. "Come on, just spill it. I know this isn't something you're happy about, but you might as well dump on me. Okay?"

"I'm not here to dump on you. I'm just surprised." Mickey sounded logical and rational, which didn't help Jessica's mood at all.

"Why? Because I found someone that actually loves me?"

"Calm down, J. I don't need the stress."

"I'm happy, Mick."

"Look, I do know you love him, and well, other than his friends, he seems nice, but come on... You're going to keep house in Alabama?"

"I've got options. He said I could even start my own business down there."

"And what might that be?"

"I could do taxes. I could pass the boards and become a CPA."

"Jess, you hate taxes."

"So?" Jessica said defiantly and then spoiled it with a sneeze.

Mickey handed her a napkin. "I rest my case."

"I'm doing this, Mick."

"I know. You've got that, 'I'll throw myself on a sword for my man' look in your eyes."

Unpleasant truths always made Jessica bitchy and sneezy. "You're jealous, aren't you? That's what this is about," she shot back, reaching for a tissue.

"Oh, that's good. Now you're just ticking me off. Poor Mickey, the brainiac. Can't keep a man, so obviously none of her friends can have one either. I don't need to listen to this. Good luck with your life, Jessica," Mickey said, handing Jessica another napkin. Then she picked up her backpack and headed out the door.

Jessica polished off her own martini, and then finished Mickey's as well and spent some time staring into the huge mirror that hung behind the bar, wishing the "I'll throw myself on a sword for my man" look never existed.

ADAM PULLED OUT his best suit and tie for the birthday party. He'd seen how nervous Jessica was, getting on her cell phone every five minutes just to make sure all details were wrapped up. Already she'd warned him that she needed to play hostess today and couldn't stay by his side all the time.

Translation: She was throwing him to the wolves.

Through the chaos of preparations, Adam managed to act calm, cool and collected.

After all, it wasn't every day he got to meet her parents.

Translation: He'd rather face a firing squad.

However, by the time they walked through the door

at the reception hall, he knew everything was going to be fine. Or at least he hoped so.

Diane, Jessica's mother, was very nice. She had sensible brown hair, wore a blue dress with matching blue shoes. She had Jessica's eyes, brown with green swirls. Eyes that were never still, always looking for something to do.

Jessica had opted to leave out the engagement news for now. "Today is Mom's day, not mine," she had said. It made sense, but he hated when she took off his ring.

The string quartet was set up in the far corner of the room. Adam had tried really hard to talk Jessica out of classical music, but his consultant's training wouldn't let him just blurt out his true opinion. He found himself leaning against a wall, sipping champagne and making small talk with Jessica's aunt Alys, spelled with a *y*, not an *i*, she stated proudly. Adam smiled encouragingly. Whatever.

Jessica's father was loads more fun than Aunt Alys. When he discovered that Adam bowled, they immediately began a discussion of the world's best bowlers. Not only that, Frank bribed one of the kitchen crew to head out for a case of beer, which he then managed to hide in the back freezer.

Eventually Frank deserted him for his union buddies, and Adam poured his beer into a champagne glass, pasted a smile on his face, and found a new corner wall to keep up.

Jessica found him there.

"How do you think it's going?" she asked, her hands twisting in front of her.

He took one of her hands and held tight. "It's going fine. Your mother looks really happy."

"Do you really mean that?"

Translation: Lie, if you don't.

"Yeah, I do," he said, which of course was a lie because her mother looked a lot like Jessica right about now.

Adam watched as Jessica's mother brought over an extra piece of cake to her aunt, and wiped up the spills when the twin girls of some cousin of Jessica's knocked over their punch cups. And when the waiter shooed her away, she began twisting her fingers nervously. Just like Jessica.

Jessica watched, too. "She was supposed to take it easy today. Not wait on everybody hand and foot."

Adam put an arm around her, pulled her into his corner. "Maybe that's what she wants to do."

Jessica still didn't look convinced. "I've failed."

She sounded so miserable and he wished there was something he could do. Instead he felt helpless. "There's no evidence to support that. Everything looks great."

"I just wanted her to have a day where somebody else could wait on her."

Adam kissed her on top of her hair. "You did good, Jess."

"I don't know."

Adam kept quiet after that. Each day, her smiles

came less and less. He had thought he knew how to make Jessica happy. But maybe he was wrong.

FIVE HOURS LATER, Jessica found her mother in the kitchen, where she was bringing in the extra dishes from the last of the party.

Immediately, Jessica removed the offending plates from her. "You aren't supposed to be working today."

"I can't just stand around while these poor people slave away."

"Aw, Ma. These poor people were paid rather well to slave away."

"And that doesn't make it right."

Jessica put down the dishes. "This was a mistake, wasn't it?"

Her mother immediately wrapped Jessica into a big hug. Something she hadn't done since Jessica was a little girl. "It was a lovely gesture, Jessica-mine."

Jessica pulled back, shaking her head. "You're just saying that, and look, you've ruined your manicure."

"Damned nail polish never stays on, anyway."

She wanted to shake her mother, but instead she just frowned. "I don't understand why you can't let somebody else take care of you."

"Ah, Jessica. That's not who I am. I'd go batty if I wasn't cooking or cleaning. It makes me feel good to take care of my family. To see other people happy."

"It does?" asked Jessica, thinking the whole thing sounded like a lot of drudge work.

Her mother picked up the dishes and began stacking them in the sink. "It's all right, dear. I don't expect you to understand."

"Why shouldn't I understand?" Jessica asked, wondering whether she had some genetic deficiency or perhaps she was just lazy.

"Because you aren't me."

Which wasn't an answer at all. "Do you think I could do that?"

"If somebody promised you a vice presidency at the end of two years, you'd probably grit your teeth and suffer through it."

Jessica laughed, but wished her mother had joked about something else. "Yeah, you're right about that. I need to go check on Adam, he looks lonely."

"He's a nice boy."

"Yeah. He is." Jessica felt for the chain that was hanging around her neck, for the Perfect Ring from the Perfect Man. Slowly, it was beginning to sink in that she wasn't the Perfect Wife.

12

JESSICA SAYS: "Mickey?"

Mickey says: "I'm not talking to you."

Jessica says: "I owe you big, big apologies. I was a bitch."

Mickey says: "Yes, you were."

Jessica says: "Can I ask you something?"

Mickey says: "Okay."

Jessica says: "If you were me, what would you do? Would you go with him, or would you give him up?"

Mickey says: "I don't know. I haven't met a man yet who would make me want to turn my life upside down, but then, I've never met a man who looks at me the way he looks at you."

Jessica says: "I don't want to give him up."

Mickey says: "Then don't."

Jessica says: "You'll be around?"

Mickey says: "Yeah. We're all here for you. You know? All for one, etsmegera, etsmegera, etsmegera."

Jessica says (as if she understands): "Thanks."

WHEN THE layoff notice came, it was blessedly sweet. Jessica had two months before her last day and would receive a severance package that provided some small comfort. She was a valued part of the team, and her contributions would be missed. Her winning spirit had helped make Hard-Wire the success that it was, yada, yada, yada.

After she was done in Artie's office, she left the building and made her way to the jogging path along the lake. And she ran. She ran until she was too exhausted to cry, ran until she couldn't think anymore. Anything to make her forget the hurt.

Yet when she was done, it was only the hurt that remained.

ON SUNDAY AFTERNOON, the Chicago Boys' and Girls' Clubs were holding the annual track and field competition. It was the day of reckoning. The team had arrived one hour early to practice and warm up. Mickey and Adam were in the stands, complete with the little Flames banners that Jessica had made for them.

Jessica was a wreck. Jasmine had misplaced her shoe and they spent thirty minutes searching for it. Sonya developed a large case of stage fright and refused to leave the bench until Jessica had convinced her that all those people in the stands were really unicorns in disguise. Christine nearly wandered off, but Adam spotted her and returned her to the appropriate place. Thank God for Latrice, who had no crisis at all.

Their race was scheduled at two o'clock. Sonya had the first leg, Jasmine would run second, Christine ran next, and then Latrice would run the anchor leg. Jessica paced back and forth going over the strategy.

"Okay, girls. This is it. The moment. The chance to go out and show the world exactly what you're made of. We've got more than a passing chance today."

"Who are we running with?" asked Christine, as if they were planning a play date.

"Not with. Against. Remember, you're out there to go faster than anyone else."

She searched the other teams, finally finding the other coach who had introduced herself earlier. She pointed. "There. That's the competition."

With a sharp eye, she appraised each girl, noting the strengths and weaknesses. The weakest runner was a smaller girl who looked too fragile to be competing, Kylie was her name according to the roster in Jessica's hand.

Jessica's heart sank. Too many times she'd been the loser herself not to know how it felt. Before she could think further, the announcer called them over to the starting line.

Jessica used the last few precious minutes to go over the baton pass and give advice on when to hold back and when to fly.

Sonya got into position, and Jessica gave her one last encouraging smile. "You can do this, Sonya."

And Sonya did. The announcer called the signals and then the starting gun was fired, and Sonya ran as if the world was behind her. Jessica had never felt so proud.

When Jasmine took off, they were only behind by a few meters. The other runner was fast, but Jasmine was catching up. As they approached the end of the stretch, she and Jasmine ran neck and neck. Jessica yelled and screamed and waved her arms, and Jasmine ended up ahead by a baton's length.

Christine ran next. She took off with a short stumble and then she was gone. They were going to win. They were going to win. They were going to win.

And then Jessica realized whom Latrice would be running against. The littlest runner. Latrice went up to the starting line to wait for Christine and the little girl lined up beside her. Latrice shot Jessica a questioning look and Jessica realized that two coaching classes and seventeen how-to books did not prepare you for moments like this. She smiled, a quickly ambivalent smile, because she really didn't have a clue how to handle it.

She looked up at Adam in the stands, found him watching her with more confidence than she felt.

It helped.

Latrice and Kylie both left the line at the same time, but it wasn't long before Latrice had a solid lead. The little girl didn't seem fazed, simply focused on the track in front of her. As she rounded the first turn, she tripped and fell, and the crowd grew silent, waiting to see what would happen now. She sat, right at the twenty-meter marker, staring up into the crowd. Latrice looked back and saw her sitting alone.

Then she turned in Jessica's direction, confused and questioning, and Jessica realized she was asking her what she should do. Jessica wondered what Mike Ditka would do, but then realized that Ditka now owned a restaurant and Jessica Barnes had opinions of her own. Good ones. Without missing a beat, she tilted her head in the smaller girl's direction and Latrice grinned with understanding.

She trotted back to where Kylie was sitting and helped her up. The crowd went wild. The smaller girl waved and began to run. She and Latrice ran together to the finish line and crossed it arm in arm.

Then all the girls ran on to the track congratulating their teammates.

It was Jessica's first meet and technically she hadn't won. She sank down on the bench, and watched closely as the girls jumped up and down and cheered each other.

Jessica, who'd never been a fan of the "as long as you play the game" motto, wondered why she felt completely unloserlike. She'd driven them and driven them and driven them, and then they...lost?

But had they? Maybe the coach had learned something today after all.

Jessica looked up into the stands and found Adam's gaze. She shrugged a what's-a-girl-to-do shrug and then he grinned at her. The sun caught her engagement ring in the light and it flashed into her eyes, and for a moment she couldn't see at all.

She loved him desperately, but it was time to face her own reality.

AFTER THE MEET was over, Adam took the team out for dinner. Quietly, Adam sat and watched Jessica bubble with enthusiasm. Watched as she gave each girl a Shirley Temple and made them toast to victory. And in general, saw her glow return.

If he hadn't been so blindly in love with her, so stupidly dead set on his own agenda, he would have noticed that she hadn't had much reason to glow recently. She looked over in his direction and gave him a happy smile, but the sad truth was that he hadn't put that smile there. Now, that responsibility lay in the hands of four little girls with a gift that he didn't have.

Tomorrow he was heading back to Alabama. A ten-hour drive, not too bad. They had decided she would stay behind this week and he would come back for her next weekend. Adam wanted to do some work on the house to make it perfect for her, but the truth was that the house would never be perfect for her.

He knew that, and he suspected she did as well.

If she noticed that he was quieter than usual, she didn't say anything, and for that he was glad. He just needed one more night with her.

He held her tight, pressing a kiss against her hair. "Jessica, I'm sorry about your job."

"It's all right. I'll be okay."

"Can I ask you something?"

She rose up on one elbow, looked him in the eyes. "Shoot."

"If you had a choice, if you could have your job back, would you?"

"Is this a hypothetical question where I can have my job back and keep you, too?"

"Yeah, it's one of those."

"Then that's an easy one. Sure."

"And if the hypothetical question was get your job back or go home with me?"

She lowered her head against his chest, a nice touch because she was no longer meeting his gaze. "I love you, Adam. Whether I'm employed or unemployed, that's not going to change."

But he noticed that she didn't answer. As a consultant, he dodged too many questions in his life not to recognize the technique. And the questions you dodged were always the tough ones.

Later, when he made love to her, every touch seemed too swift, every kiss seemed too short. Afterward, he held her close, unable to sleep. Instead he lay awake, memorizing the feel of her skin, the sounds of her even breathing, and basking in the warm glow that only belonged to her.

ABOUT 5:00 P.M., Adam hit Kentucky, just about the same time he realized he'd made an error in judgment.

His conscience had been eerily quiet on the trip and it took four strong cups of coffee for him to come to grips with the fact that there were options that he had chosen to ignore. Options that would keep Jessica in

Chicago. Where she belonged. He might not be able to rectify everything in the world, but damned if he wasn't going to give it his best shot.

By the time he hit Nashville, he had talked to Osterson twice. The first time Osterson had wished him luck. The second time Osterson realized just how serious Adam was.

When he pulled into his driveway at Valley Head, he pulled out his computer and went to work.

On Sunday afternoon he ran into the first roadblock. JCN had just recently acquired another software company and had already taken a hit on earnings from that one. With the Hard-Wire acquisition, they couldn't afford any duplication of function anywhere.

Damn. Adam spent all day Monday on the phone with JCN's head of finance. It was the same story.

He scoured the financial report and the latest org chart, but everywhere he looked, he ran into the same unavoidable truth.

JCN didn't need Hard-Wire's finance department at all.

ON SUNDAY MORNING, Jessica packed up her *Better Homes & Garden* books. She told herself it was because her apartment was too small for her to lay them out, but in her heart she knew the truth.

The day of reckoning at Hard-Wire was set for the week after July fourth. Jessica reached for a tissue. Lately she hadn't gone anywhere without one.

Her résumé needed just a couple more lines to be perfect, and then, off to meet with headhunters. Gee.

Her apartment was now full of Adam. He was everywhere she looked. She could picture him laughing on her couch, typing away at his computer in her office. Yes, she could picture him everywhere in Chicago. And why were they going to Alabama?

The answer was that they weren't. Or at least, she wasn't.

Time for Jessica to realize she could never be happy living someone else's life. It would kill all possible options for a happily-ever-after for her and Adam.

Even the thought gave her shivers.

She went to the office and packed up the cookbooks she'd bought, the home-decorating books she'd bought, and all the articles she'd printed from a how-to Web site.

Finally she was done, but when she walked into the bathroom to take her shower, the towel she picked up smelled like his cologne and the extra toothbrush he'd brought was lying next to hers.

She turned on the water until it steamed the walls, stepped under the hot spray, and then, Jessica broke down and cried.

ADAM WAS CONVINCED there had to be something somewhere. He just needed to find it.

By Thursday, he was ready to give up. Instead, he called Jessica. She sounded quieter than usual and told him they had some things to discuss when he got back. He tried to get it out of her, but she wouldn't budge. Then he tried to rile her up, talking about how the Packers were going to stomp all over the Bears. But even that, a traditional Chicago war cry, didn't merit a bit of distress.

He steered the conversation toward Hard-Wire finances. When she discussed the third-quarter revenues, the value proposition became crystal clear. In his excitement, he hung up on her, but immediately he called back, said he loved her, and hung up again.

It would be a tough sell, but he could do it. He flew up and back on Sunday to meet with Garrison Reynolds, to go over exactly what inroads Hard-Wire had made in Asia-Pacific.

He couldn't let Jessica know what he was doing. Odds were, he was going to fail. If he disappointed her, he wouldn't be able to live with himself.

By the following week, he'd had ten hours of sleep, forty-three pots of coffee, and one mighty fine PowerPoint presentation that his future depended on.

He drove up and met with Osterson. Showed him the pitch. Osterson shook his head in disbelief. "It just might work, but I got to warn you, you screw up this deal, and it's your ass, son."

Right now his job was the least of his worries. Adam smiled. "Not an issue."

Next on the agenda was convincing Artie Boodlesman that an out-and-out takeover might not be in his best interest. That was a trickier line to walk. Artie had poured his heart and savings into Hard-Wire. How much was he willing to gamble? He heard Adam out, bombarded him with question after question, and Adam was prepared for each one. Finally, Artie was convinced.

The last leg in the triangle was JCN itself. Osterson set up the meeting with JCN for Thursday in San Jose. The entire business development team was there, and Adam had asked that JCN's sales and marketing group be invited as well.

And that day Adam made the presentation of his life. He had used the 2002 and 2003 sales figures to show what progress Hard-Wire had made into the AP market. He had distributor names and client lists, and it ran like the Who's Who of the Pacific Rim.

It was the exact market that JCN had been trying to crack for the last five years. Unfortunately for JCN, a Korean firm had a stranglehold on the situation, but because of its small size, Hard-Wire had slipped in where JCN could not.

The answer wasn't for Hard-Wire to be assimilated into JCN, the answer was for JCN to buy a stake in Hard-Wire, let Hard-Wire forge the way into Asia Pacific, and then, and only then, would Hard-Wire be branded with the JCN logo, corporate umbrella, and all the other accoutrements that came with ownership.

The BD guys were nodding in appreciation, the sales vice-president looked intrigued and just a little bit greedy. From men who never gave anything away, this was progress indeed.

The real test would be over dinner. Adam and Osterson took them to Emile's for dinner, and Adam took every question, handling it with finesse, crafting the perfect answer, and volleying it back to the recipient, all the while keeping the wineglasses filled. His smile never wavered, not even when he was sure the deal would tank.

But in the end he was wrong.

AFTER THE prelim agreements had been signed, Osterson took Adam into his office.

"Taylor, I've never seen anything like that. You've got a future here. But I have one question for you. Why? Why screw up the known by gambling on the unknown? It's a solid strategy, and JCN bit on it, but a man's got to be dumber than a sack of hair to pull his hand at the last minute like that."

Adam felt the wired buzz of too much caffeine and too little sleep, and he rubbed eyes that were way too dry. Still he could smile. "If I'm going to fail, I'm going to fail by daring greatly."

Osterson's eyes narrowed. "Some day when you fail greatly, your career won't survive."

Adam picked up his briefcase and made his way to the door, his step lighter than it had been in a long, long time. "Then that's a career not worth having, sir," he answered back.

Adam had respected Osterson for most of his tenure, but maybe, just maybe, it was time for a change.

ADAM SPENT his last night in his house. He wandered from room to room, for the first time seeing empty spaces rather than fanciful dreams. The quiet chirping of the crickets called from outside; all the rest of the world was at rest.

He packed up his bags and left the paperwork on the kitchen counter for the real estate agent, then went to say his last goodbye.

He brought flowers with him to the cemetery. Not because they were his mother's favorite or anything, mainly because he wanted to give her something, but had never been able to.

"Sorry, Ma," he said. As a conversation starter, it wasn't much. He'd always had great plans for taking care of his mother, setting her up in fine style, but he was fast discovering that, as a planner, he really sucked.

He placed the flowers on her grave and closed his eyes, trying to conjure her up one more time.

He waited, but there was only silence. It wasn't hard to imagine what she'd tell him.

Why would you be apologizing to me? You've finally found your own way now.

"You're still gonna be around, right?" he whispered to himself. Carefully he listened, waiting for her wisecracks or extravagant sighs, but all he heard was the far-off call of the whippoorwill. Once, twice, three times. No answers, only the call of the damned bird.

Adam got to his feet and took one last look.

And he never looked back again.

ON SATURDAY MORNING, it was hell just getting out of bed. The phone rang, but Jessica refused to answer it.

She hadn't seen a human being for three days, and right now, she didn't want to.

She'd rehearsed her speech over and over in her head, but she always got to the "I can't marry you" part, and couldn't get any further. Adam was supposed to be back in Chicago tomorrow. Twenty-four hours to figure out how to turn down the most perfect man she'd ever met.

She was heading for the bathroom when her doorbell rang. Jessica looked at the grungy T-shirt she was wearing and debated answering it. But then the doorbell rang again, and she dragged herself to the door.

It was Adam.

Oh, God, she still hadn't gotten her speech right and she looked like crap.

But he didn't seem to care. He walked in, looking a little uncertain himself.

"Did Garrison call you?"

Jessica, trying to understand why Garrison would have called, shook her head.

"JCN's not going to buy Hard-Wire."

Jessica sank down on the couch. "Is this a joke?"

"No. Eventually they will, but right now they're just buying a majority stake. Jessica, you're going to keep your job. There probably will be a takeover, but not for several years. You've got some time now."

She sat there, waiting for the buoyant, gleeful moment where she would burst out in joyful song, but the lead weight in her heart stayed firm. She didn't feel anything at all.

He was watching her expectantly, and because she knew the part she was supposed to play, she smiled. "Good."

Adam stayed near the door, opting not to touch her, not to hold her. It was probably for the best, but still her leg began to shake.

"Well, okay, you're taking that well," he said. "I brought something for you. I don't need it anymore and I thought you might want it."

He handed her a little heart key ring with one key. A car key. A Porsche car key.

This jarred her awake far more than the job ever could and she blinked at him. "I can't take your car."

"It was never my car. I always wanted to give it to somebody else, and I think that's meant to be you. I can get a Honda or something."

"No, I really can't take your car," she insisted, wishing he wouldn't make this so damned difficult.

"Well, okay, maybe I shouldn't have sprung that on you right now. Let's table that. There's one more thing."

He pulled a Cubbies hat from behind his back and put it on his head. "This one's for me, Jess."

He looked so nervous, so uncertain, and she, the queen of poor timing, blurted out the one thing she'd been practicing all weekend, but could never get right. "I can't marry you."

Instantly the uncertainty was gone. He sat down beside her. "I bet I can make you change your mind," he said in a voice that was not nearly as cocky as usual.

She closed her eyes, tried to keep going. She needed to get through this. This was the one time she couldn't afford to screw up. "No, you don't understand. I thought I could do all this, go away to Alabama, but it was just like when I ran away before. After seven hours, I'd be right back home."

It didn't seem to faze him at all. He pulled her close against him. "I know. I'm not asking you to leave, Jessica."

She raised her head, and listened very carefully. "What do you mean?" she asked, thinking she must have been mistaken.

"I want to live here. In Chicago. Preferably with you, if that's okay?"

And there it was. The load off her heart. It was gone. She drew in deep mouthfuls of air. The questions came pouring out. "You're going to be based in Chicago, then? What about your house?"

"They have houses in Chicago?" he asked.

"Yeah."

"That'll work. And I've got one more thing to tell you. I quit. I've got some feelers out, and I don't think it'll take me very long to be gainfully employed again. But right now I'm the unemployed one in the family."

She blinked, trying to reconcile Adam with unemployed. "You quit?" she asked. But he looked so happy, so content. And then she got it. "It was all that talk about living your dreams, wasn't it? You never did say what yours was. What do you want to do? Paint? Do some consulting on your own?''

She was babbling, but he didn't seem to mind.

''Well, it's not exactly my dream, but I figure I put thirty-five-thousand people out of work. If I can get rid of thirty-five-thousand jobs, surely I can create thirty-five-thousand jobs. I'm thinking I could be really good at it. And I've got some ideas.''

To Jessica, it sounded completely mundane. After all that talk about making a difference, living what you want. She felt sure he was missing something here. ''But this is your big chance. Now you could go after your dreams.''

He pulled her to him and his mouth came whisper-close. She knew it was exactly where he belonged. ''You know what, Jess? I've got my dream right here.''

* * * * *

Don't miss the next installment
of the BACHELORETTE PACT
from Kathleen O'Reilly!
IT SHOULD HAPPEN TO YOU
is coming in April 2004…

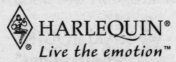

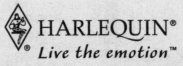